GOLDEN SOLE

The Leaf

CLINTON CAMPBELL

For my wife, Lisa.
We've been through so much together.

Contents

GOLDEN SOLE

One

Felix Arlen studied his gold and black uniform in the mirror and distantly noted that his hat was quite crooked, he fixed it with a moment's effort before letting out a sigh. He knew that he couldn't delay any further, as his shift started in less than a minute so instead, he turned on the spot and slowly made his way across the room to place his hand on the door handle. Felix hesitated for a moment, unable to help himself before taking a few deep breaths and then slowly letting them out. Felix was left in a state of calm, where all his tension had vanished, and he was left feeling calm, collected, and empty of fear. Felix opened the door before taking a single step outside and his tranquillity shattered like it was the most fragile thing in the world.

The lobby of the hotel was brightly lit with twinkling chandeliers and stylish pillars lining the walls, all made from dark stone. The marble floor glinted in the bright lights, it's surface perfectly smooth and polished immaculately. The large metal doors of the elevators shone back at it, having been cleaned this morning. The lobby was just as pretty as the first thousand times he had seen it, the reason for his lost calm was the numerous people entering and exiting the building.

That was always the same, bellhops, cleaners, security, and more wandered the floor, attending to their duties while customers came and left from the glass frontage of the building. All of the early risers ready to head out and go about their business for the day. Felix spotted George, a fellow bellhop, pushing a luggage trolley towards the elevators accompanied by two elderly ladies dressed in pantsuits who tittered at him as they passed. Felix realized he had been standing still for a rather long while now, long enough for somebody to notice and he immediately felt humiliation twist in his stomach.

Felix gathered himself as best he could and turned to head to the drop off zone, located at the front of the hotel, where guests were arriving and leaving. He barely made it a foot towards his destination before he ran straight into an outstretched hand and he took a step backward to avoid collision with the offending limb. Felix turned to find a tall, impeccably dressed man watching him with a look of disdain on his face.

"Not watching where you are going, Arlen?" Alistair asked sharply.

Felix swallowed down the flash of anger that cut through him and took another step backward. Alistair was a concierge, who also worked in the Golden Salt Hotel, and someone Felix tended to do his best to avoid during his shifts. Unfortunately, it didn't seem he would be able to avoid him today, as Alistair was staring directly at him. Felix almost flinched at the feeling of the man's attention and did his best to crush any sign of a reaction on his face, he made sure to drop his gaze to watch the man's mouth.

"I guess not," Felix said quietly, crossing his arms in front of him like a shield between them.

The contrast between them was interesting, Felix thought. Alistair's body language screamed professionalism and complete confidence in himself. Felix's own was much more closed off, and unsure.

"At least you aren't late," Alistair added when the silence edged towards awkward.

Felix frowned at him and used the feeling of annoyance like a weapon to force himself he felt to speak up.

"I am *never* late," Felix said quietly, in his defense.

Alistair studied him for a long moment before suddenly stepping around him and striding off without another comment. Felix glanced over his shoulder in time to catch Alistair speaking charmingly to a guest that was looking relieved for the help. Felix watched the man for a moment, as much as he personally disliked him, there was no doubt that Alistair had an impressive ability to engage and connect with people. He knew the right things to say, and the right times to say them to get the most out of every exchange with someone. It seemed to even equip him to deal with his superiors with little effort, but when it came to anyone below Alistair on the totem pole, his silver tongue was quick to turn sharp, he could and would cut you down verbally at the drop of a hat for the smallest perceived mistake or inefficiency.

What felt worse was that Felix had worked at the hotel for years before Alistair had even applied to work here as a Bellhop. Alistair had, with seeming ease, quickly outstripped everyone around him to land where he now resided within the hotel's hierarchy. Felix didn't know where the man drew his confidence from, the kind of confidence that allowed him to easily place himself above others and condescend to those he saw beneath him. The man held no fear of reprisal or repercussion from his words; all carefully chosen to inflict some measure of negative impact on his targets.

Felix sighed at where his thoughts had taken him, the same old circle of negativity that would drag him down for days. Felix opened one of the many glass doors at the front of the hotel and let in a man and woman before surreptitiously studying their clothing as they stepped over the threshold.

Old grey suit for the man, some loose threads near his collar, his tie was crooked as well. The woman was wearing a pantsuit and some small amount of jewelry was visible. Young, well-dressed but not wealthy.

The man and the woman thanked him as they passed, and he allowed the door to shut behind them before Felix mumbled hello and stepped forward to take their luggage. He placed it on the nearest available trolley and moved to follow them as they headed towards the front counter. Felix stood a distance away while they spoke to Alice, a tall thin woman with a long nose, one of the many receptionists employed by the hotel.

Felix waited quietly, watching the three of them exchange Smalltalk and clamped down on the twinge of alarm he felt when the man laughed suddenly. Alice stood from her chair to unlock the cabinet behind her and grabbed a tiny key off a hook, the numbers were too far away for him to read, and the tiny font didn't help, but Felix managed to spot the newly created gap on the hooks before she slid the cabinet door closed; six down, four across.

Cabinet one, room six-zero-four.

Felix watched as they continued talking and this time when the woman laughed he was ready for the sudden noise. The two guests stepped away from the counter and turned back towards him. When they approached, Felix turned the trolley towards the elevators and started to push without a word. Felix entered the elevator first and moved the trolley to the back and out of the way so that the other two had enough space to step inside.

The door shut behind them and they were facing him, so Felix turned to face the trolley, pretending to straighten the luggage. They spoke to each other during the short trip upwards, and with each passing moment, Felix became more aware of his heart thudding in his chest. The man laughed at something the woman had said and Felix's ears burned, certain that it had to have been at his expense but somehow having heard none of the words. Humiliation welled up but he fought it down.

His anxiety was surging up despite his best efforts, he knew logically that they hadn't been laughing at him, or even talking about him at all, but he couldn't help the reaction, he'd been this way for a long time now, and it only seemed to get worse with every passing day. He would feel an awful pressure build up inside his chest, rising like the tide and making him feel hyperaware of everything around him.

Felix knew he was reading far too deeply into every action other people would make, but at the moment it felt like every action people took was part of some hidden narrative to strike at him through manipulation or calculated words. It had crushed any form of connection he could ever have made with others, he had ended up drawing away from his friends and it had killed any longing to repair them or even wanting to make any more. Felix had resorted to seeking out interaction on the internet, away from the crushing pressure he felt every time someone so much as glanced his way, he would seek out others there, and sometimes he wouldn't feel as if he were so crushingly alone.

Felix glanced at the two in the elevator with him before returning to stare at the luggage, as if it might run away should he remove his attention from it for even an instant.

Would they ask him something soon? Did they think him rude for not facing them, for not speaking to them? Was he making them feel awkward? Would they report him to management for acting unsightly? A surge of guilt joined the panic, would they accuse him of something, or tell a member of staff about him? It would be their word against his, two against one. Felix managed to crush the panic down when he remembered the cameras, everything was being watched, it would be fine, he hadn't done anything at all, he forced himself to take a quiet but deep breath, making sure to keep his shoulders and chest locked to hide the motion.

Something like that had happened before; only a simple complaint, that he had made a guest feel awkward when he didn't speak up, but nothing had ever come of it. A verbal warning, from his then superior, to present better to the guests to avoid any more complaints in the future.

They had never written anything down, and the boss that had overseen those complaints had long since retired. He'd had a clean slate at present, and he wanted it to stay that way.

Felix felt a flash of anger cut through his chest at the elevators speed, the ride seemed to drag on forever. With every word the two guests spoke to each other, Felix could feel his anxiousness building, even more, he could almost see hidden insults directed his way and he had to reassure himself that they were talking about someone else, they didn't even know him. The elevating dinged and the noise dragged Felix out of the panic, as they stepped out of the elevator and away from him.

Felix took another deep breath and rolled the trolley out into the hall, before turning right. He moved past where they had stopped in the hall, and in the direction that would lead them to the door, six-zero-four. He stopped in front of it and almost breathed a sigh of relief as the task was almost finished. Felix glanced over and accidentally caught the woman's eye and immediately noticed that they were both looking at him strangely, the panic returned greater than before.

"How did you know which room was ours?" The woman asked curiously. "You didn't even ask which one it was."

The woman's curiosity felt more like suspicion to him, and she pulled out the keys from her handbag and dangled them in front of her like a cat with a toy, a tiny back '604' was written on the tag. The man nodded and made a 'hmm' noise, scrunching up his face in thought. Felix forced himself to speak up.

"Alice, the receptionist told me in advance," Felix said quietly.

"Of course, how silly of me." She laughed easily.

The man noised out another 'hmm' but much more loudly than before and shook his head at her obnoxiously, the woman swatted him on the arm looking amused. The man nodded at Felix in thanks, and the two began taking the luggage into their room.

The door shut behind them when they had finished and Felix slowly moved back the way he'd come, taking his time, savoring the silence and solitude of the now-empty hall. The awful feelings that had overtaken him were vanishing slowly on the trip back and when he finally stepped back inside the elevator, he was relieved to find it empty. Felix pressed the button for the lobby and listened as it hummed when the floor ticked down to the first floor, he took a deep breath and let it out slowly.

The door opened with a ding and Felix stepped out into the lobby, ready to do it all over again.

Grant Lewis, the Bell captain, and Felix's direct superior pulled him aside sometime later and told him that he would be interviewing the next batch of potentials later this afternoon. Grant wanted Felix to come with him, so he had someone to get a second point of view from; the hotel had become very picky about who it hired these days after a messy lawsuit with one of the previous hires and as a result, the hiring decisions weren't made at all lightly. Felix mumbled his agreement quietly. This wasn't something new for him, It was something that had occurred nearly every time someone quit.

Originally, years ago now, Grant had been the one trying for the bell-hop position, and Felix had sat in on that batch of interviews as well, alongside the previous Bell captain. Felix still didn't know why the old Captain had picked him to do it, but it had become almost routine at this point. It was funny Felix thought, that now Grant had been promoted to bell captain, and he was still just a bellhop.

Believe it or not, Felix wasn't bitter, Grant was a decent guy; he did his work, he adjusted shifts for emergency's without too much complaining and he never acted on a guest's complaints in haste. Felix could at least take heart in the fact that Alistair had been promoted laterally out of being a bellhop before Felix had ever had the chance to work under him; Felix might've taken a one-way trip to the roof of the hotel if that had been the case.

When his shift finally ended, Felix headed off to the changing room to get out of his uniform and into black business slacks and a black dress shirt with the hotel's logo on it. He spent a moment tidying himself in the mirror and made his way out of the room and towards a section of the building on the first floor that held some office space. Felix spotted the small conference room that was attached to a waiting room filled with chairs, the area hidden out of view of the main hotel lobby by a large divider.

The waiting and conference rooms were empty of people, save for himself. The conference room existed for the management to handle things that a simple bellhop would have no reason to be included on, so he didn't know what it was used for, but it also happened to be where the job interviews were conducted.

The room itself was dominated by a large black oval table and a whiteboard built into the wall at the far side while black leather chairs lined the table. Grant wasn't there yet and probably wouldn't be for another hour, so he let himself into the conference room and found a seat on the opposite side furthest from the door, taking care not to sit at the head of the table. Felix placed his head down on the table and did his best to cherish the silence.

Nearly an hour later Grant finally appeared, leading a small group of men and woman through the hotel lobby and into the waiting room, once they were all seated Grant spoke to them for a brief moment, likely reassuring them before he entered the conference room and shut the door behind him. Grant sat down next to Felix with a loud drawn-out sigh.

"That bad?" Felix asked quietly, as close to at ease as he had been all day.

"I'm just being a drama queen," Grant replied tiredly.

Felix didn't feel quite as worried with people he had known for a long time or those he had spent a great deal of time around. Funnily enough, if a person was acting openly hostile, or presented themselves as an adversary of sorts his anxiousness dropped a great deal, which wasn't much help, as actively hostile people were few and far between.

Felix had long since figured out part of the problem if he didn't know how a person would respond to him; his imagination would run wild and his body would quickly drag itself into a fight or flight response. If he spent a great deal of time around a person or interacted with them regularly, he would slowly be able to map out a series of expected responses from them and he didn't feel like they would suddenly attack him for a perceived mistake.

Felix had noticed that people rarely did things, in a workplace environment at least, that exceeded those responses by too much, unless they were under great amounts of pressure, panic, stress, anger, or excitement. Felix figured he could avoid them when they deviated too greatly from the mental model that he built of them. It didn't always work, unfortunately; you couldn't always avoid people you worked with; in fact, it was impossible in some cases.

Felix did his best to mitigate his anxiety, to overcome the need to crawl up into a ball and hide from the world. None of these tricks helped when the situation involved people he had never met, or only recently became acquaintances, like when the guests entered the hotel, which was only every single working day.

"Alright," Grant said, "We have a total of four people applying, two for Bellhop, two for receptionist."

Felix nodded but hesitated before speaking.

"Receptionist?" Felix prompted quietly.

They were usually put through a different interview process by one of the upper managers. Grant's job as bell captain usually only required him to hire people that worked directly below him. Had whoever usually hired the receptionist handed off the job to Grant?

"Oh, Darcy; the guy who usually does it is still on long service leave. I have to fill in for the next couple of weeks." Grant explained tiredly.

Felix nodded in understanding before dropping the subject to avoid annoying him further. There was only one position for each role at the hotel, one receptionist, and one bellhop. Only four candidates were in the waiting room, two for each position most likely. The hotel tended to only hire female counter staff and male bellhops, if this was sexist or not Felix wasn't sure. The two women in the waiting room were likely here for the reception job, and likewise the men for the bellhop position.

Grant messed with his phone for a moment before finally turning it off and standing up. He went to the door and opened it.

"Steven?" Grant called pleasantly, "Please come on through."

Grant held the door open and the man who was presumably Steven, stepped through, he didn't look at all surprised to see Felix at the table which meant that Grant must have warned them that he would be sitting in. Grant shut the door and directed Steven to a seat, before sitting himself across from the man at the large table.

Felix had a good angle off to the side to look straight down the length of it at them both. Steven was an older man, late forties at his best guess. His clothes were professional but well worn. He had mid-length hair that just brushed his shoulders and a full but maintained beard. He would have to shave it off for the job, if he refused, he would likely be quickly denied. The image was everything to the hotel.

Steven's body language wasn't confident exactly, although it held a lot of the hallmarks of a confident person, he wasn't insecure either. It was a combination he had seen before in people who had taken many interviews and rarely gotten callbacks. It bordered on uncaring or indifferent; he had one leg laying over his knee at the ankle. He presented good responses, well-practiced which showed that he was used to the interview process, and he spoke with a level voice at a steady pace, completely unrushed. Steven had good social skills, and from the man's answers, he was likely looking for a long-term role, which was exactly the kind of thing they wanted. Steven had no higher education, other than a high school certificate but it didn't matter for a bellhop.

Felix turned to study Grant for a moment, he seemed more distant than normal, tired, and distracted, but it wasn't the interview that was responsible, he had noticed it earlier as well; something was weighing on him. Steven may have noticed at some point because he began to show signs of closing off, thinking he was already unlikely to get the job. Grant would in turn see that as a lack of enthusiasm and think that Steven was just going through the motions of the interview, answering by rote.

When they finished the interview, Grant stood and shook Steven's hand. They exchanged pleasantries and he led him out the door, Grant returned and made some quick notes on his pad of paper and flipped it over to a fresh page. Steven wouldn't be making the shortlist unless the other candidate was truly terrible.

If Felix had to go through this process now, he knew he wouldn't have a chance of being hired again. He had only gotten in because his father had known one of the people who were responsible for hiring new employees years ago. Felix's father and mother had both long since passed, and the man who had hired him no longer worked at the hotel. Nepotism wouldn't help him a second time, Felix knew.

Grant brought the next person in immediately, and it was a woman this time, in her mid-twenties. She was smiling brightly, but she was hunching her shoulders slightly, trying to make herself smaller; she was nervous, worried, and anxious but had it under control. Her feet were pointed at the captain, and she leaned forward to engage him easily; she was eager and directed all her attention at the captain.

Her top button was also undone, and Felix dragged his eyes away from it, annoyed at himself.

She was energetic; but nervous, she fumbled some of her words, but wasn't embarrassed by the mistakes; laughing at herself easily, she was resilient. The captain would probably note the fumbling down as a mark against her communication score, but Felix didn't see it as anything that would truly hamper her when communicating with guests. It would be a mark against her though even if a small one, the hotel didn't want to hire someone that would give the guests a poor image.

Her foot was jumping lightly on the floor, indicated excitement or high tension, probably both. She was also doing something with her eyes, switching her gaze between Grant's left and right eye every few seconds; it made them catch the light. She was enthusiastic and optimistic; she would likely be a positive influence on the other staff members once she integrated. She was a good choice for short midterm and would likely be promoted into a sales role or even a concierge, once she began to refine her social skills and grew into the role.

Grant thanked her, seemingly pleased with the interview, and wrote down some quick notes then brought the next one in, another man this time, tall, fit, good looking, and his shoulders were held back naturally, real confidence that wasn't faked. He was also noticeably younger; Felix would put him at nineteen at most. He answered all the questions without a problem, he was quick-witted and sharp of mind. He handled the back and forth well, didn't derail the interview in any way, and he was focused.

He didn't offer anything without being asked, however, and his posture was sending up red flags, the man was sprawled slightly in the chair, owning his environment, it was a calculated show of confidence. One of his feet was aimed at the door which indicated he didn't want to be here, but he maintained eye contact perfectly and deferred to Grant's responses several times which showed he would likely be able to take directions. Now and then he would glance out the window, or at Felix.

He would be a perfect fit, but he was also showing signs that he didn't want to be here. Was he pressured to apply for the job? It could be, at his young age but it didn't feel quite right. He might have seen the job as a bellhop as beneath him. Glancing at the copy of his resume sitting in front of Felix revealed some more details, he was a high achiever. He likely wanted a position somewhere higher up the food chain at the hotel. Which would make this his method of getting a foot in the door, would try to get promoted up and out of the position quickly. If that did happen, he wouldn't be here for long if it didn't, he might just leave. He probably wouldn't be a long-term solution for a bellhop. Grant had noticed his affected lack of care midway through the interview and pushed him a bit with the questions as a test, but he got through completely unscathed.

Grant walked him to the door and made some more notes before he brought in the last person, a woman, sharp features, severe expression. Late thirties early forties, polished social skills, good posture, confident, and easily maintained eye contact with the captain. Grant seems a little bit intimidated, as this woman appears as if she comes from somewhere far higher up the food chain then a simple bell captain like Grant.

Grant fumbled a question and the woman titters at him, he's flagging now, is completely off his game, and slightly embarrassed at the mistake. Grant shifts and now his feet are pointed at the door. The woman is forceful, direct, and focused, it seemed calculated but still genuine to a degree, she has used her body language as a weapon throughout the interview. Probably the best candidate by far for a receptionist but Grant will likely choose someone else because of the embarrassment.

A miscalculation on her part perhaps but she would be shortlisted for the next open receptionist spot, or more likely a Concierge. Grant led her to the door, and she vanished out of the room and through the lobby, the waiting room was empty now when Grant returned to sprawl in his chair and let out another long sigh before marking down a few more things.

Grant, Felix noted once more, had been a bit off lately, tired and stressed, it had become more noticeable after he finished talking with someone from upper management last week. Grant was either going to be promoted laterally into a management role, which this most recent hiring task pointed at, or he was thinking of resigning due to pressure from above. Felix wondered who was going to get Grant's job if he did leave, It certainly wouldn't be the first time Felix was passed over, the turnover rate at this place was obscene, how he had managed to keep his job for this long Felix would probably never know.

"Well, what do you think?" Grant asked tiredly, looking at him from his seat.

Felix watched him quietly for a moment before he spoke up.

Felix opened the door to his apartment and stepped inside. He could almost physically feel the tension vanish from his body, the walls around him feeling like a shield between him and a world filled with people. He strode over to his bed and immediately flopped face-first onto it, content to do nothing until his body forced him into motion again.

The apartment was small, and it was not much more than a single multi-purpose room; a small kitchen, with a white rolling divider wall that stretched from floor to ceiling, blocked off the kitchen from the bedroom, there was a single door that led to the attached bathroom, with only a shower and toilet inside. A cheap couch lay against a flat space of wall opposite his computer, perched on a desk. The apartment was cheap, functional and he made sure to keep it neat and tidy.

Felix had noticed over the years, that his mental state worsened the messier his living situation became and keeping it as free of clutter as he could defiantly help alleviate some of the stress. Eventually, he was forced to get up and use the bathroom; so he peeled off the clothes he had worn to the interview and placed them into a basket to be washed in the morning.

While most people would be getting ready to go out on a Friday and find adventures within the ample nightlife in the city, Felix had quite different plans. He would eat his dinner, browse the internet for several hours, play video games and then go to bed, it was the same pattern that he had followed for years and he had found no compelling reason for him to change it. He had many acquaintances, but he had no friends; he wasn't a part of any social group or activities and he didn't have any hobbies.

Playing video games had once filled the spot of a hobby for him, and he still did it almost every day, but like most things, in life, he found that he now experienced no joy, happiness, or feeling of accomplishment from it. He simply continued out of habit, having spent so much time doing it, it was something he was good at if only because he had become so very well-practiced, the sunk cost fallacy urged him ever onwards.

Felix ate his dinner, browsed the internet for hours, played video games, and then went to bed, the pattern remained unbroken.

Felix stared out of his apartment window at all of the people walking the streets. This Saturday morning was slightly different than most, as there was a political march taking place in the city today, apparently in about an hour, and the crowds of people had already started flooding into the streets to attend it. These types of things had been becoming more common in recent years, more people able to organize and form groups, and those groups spreading the information even further online, social media at its most effective.

This march was for bringing about free higher education for everyone; it was an interesting topic. Felix wondered if he had been able to afford to go to university back when he was still amidst his education, would he have gone? and If he had gone, what would his life have been like? Would he have become a different person than he was now, perhaps without all his social problems and hang-ups?

He didn't know, he doubted it though.

Felix had noted that life tended to follow the same patterns over and again and without a massive change, it would continue set in its ways. Something else would have come along and knocked him down, he would still have distanced himself from others physically and closed himself off emotionally. He would have still ended up right where he was now, only he would have a higher paying job, he supposed and could buy more useless things that brought him no joy.

Perhaps he could have bought a better apartment, a bigger one even. Felix didn't even feel bad about it, not really. When Felix was on his own, he didn't feel much of anything, he just felt empty and void of anything at all. He didn't hold any bitterness, hate, jealousy, or anger for others; He felt nothing but indifference. There was no motivation to improve his situation, he just existed in the hole that he had dug for himself, never even bothering to lift his head and stare up at the sky.

He had done it to himself, forced himself not to feel anything to protect himself from being hurt and vulnerable, but he had become so good at wearing it, that he had seemingly become the amour. Years later now, it just sapped him of any positive feelings entirely and the amour had become startling fragile when he had to interact with other people.

Felix couldn't imagine a more useless form of protection.

He was watching one of the many live streams of the march, and the reporter walked confidently down the main street with her camera crew a step behind her, talking about everything without a shred of hesitation. People waved at the camera in passing, with smiles on their faces, happy to be a part of something they deemed so important.

Felix wondered idly about what it would feel like to join them, to feel so strongly about something that he might even act to advocate for it? He hadn't ever been to anything like it, so he couldn't simulate the experience in his mind, at least not accurately. Felix tried to imagine being inside the crowd of people, all with goals that had enough meaning to drive them out onto the streets to cry out for what they wanted amongst like-minded individuals. He wondered what it would be like to stand among them, nobody knowing who he was, or why he was there, to be among people who felt so strongly and to be a part of something.

Surprisingly, Felix didn't feel a rising surge of panic at the thought he found he almost wanted to go. Felix watched the Livestream for a while longer, but the thought had remained stuck in his mind. Felix could go, join the march and do something, nobody he knew would be there, and if they were it would be impossible for them to find him, and nobody would be expecting anything from him; he would be just another random nobody among a crowd of tens of thousands.

Felix noted that his foot was jumping against the floor, and he stared at it, he was excited, Felix couldn't remember the last time he had felt excited about anything at all. He checked the time on his computer and then found the bus schedule taped to his wall. The next bus into downtown left in fifteen minutes and Felix decided that he was going to be on it.

The bus was running late, and with the number of people that were traversing the streets; it had resulted in an impossible to keep a schedule for even the most diligent of bus drivers. All they could do was soldier on and try not to fall any further behind; but when even that failed, they were content to just soldier on.

The march was starting on the east side of the city and cutting through the main strip to the west. Felix lived on the west side but fairly central, and it was a thirty-minute bus ride, during normal traffic to cross the city. It would likely take him an hour, at least, to get there with all the people interrupting the flow of traffic. He decided on a compromise, he would ride the bus to the central business district, wait on the main strip for the march to reach the halfway point and then slip into the crowd. The march would reach its endpoint only a few blocks away from his apartment anyway, how convenient.

The bus came into view from around a corner, taking another minute to wait for the pedestrians to cross in front of it, it drove through the traffic lights and paused in front of Felix at the bus stop. The doors opened and a deluge of people spilled out chatting to each other, heads turning to take in the area. Once they had cleared to the entrance, he joined the newly formed queue to enter the bus.

Felix started to feel the panic well up; as the person who was standing behind Felix jostled him. He bumped into the woman in front of him and immediately held himself rigid and made sure to allow a noticeable gap form between them. The woman didn't turn around and Felix released the breath he had been holding. When he was at the front of the queue, Felix tapped his card on the machine and stepped further into the bus.

Still mostly empty, with Felix having been near the front of the line, he made sure to take a window seat near the back of the bus so he could avoid the gaze of anyone by looking out the window. Once all the occupants on the bus were dealt with the doors closed and the bus started forward with a hissing noise. The front of the bus dipped alarmingly deep into the oncoming lane before straightening back onto the correct side of the street.

Felix stared out the window and watched the city pass by.

Saltwall City was a metropolis, and skyscrapers pierced the sky in the hundreds. It was a very densely populated city, something like seven million people lived here. A series of trains ran under the city while buses and taxi's dominated the streets, ferrying people back and forth. Felix lost his train of thought for a moment when he spotted his workplace peeking over the top of another building in the distance.

The 'Golden Salt' hotel had its name spelled across the top of the building in large golden stylized letters, golden tracery and highlights broke up the dark glass of the building. It was forty-nine floors tall, an absolute goliath of a building. Felix watched it for a moment before it was cut off from view by another building.

Felix had lived in this city for most of his life, having moved here with his parents when he was only a child. His father had been offered a management job in the very same hotel, around about when Felix had been at high school age. Felix himself had been hired to work as a bellhop through a friend his father had made while working there. His father had used that connection at the first chance he had, and Felix had been there ever since. But when Felix had turned nineteen both of his mother and father had died in a car accident, the cause of which determined as a no-fault collision.

Felix missed them greatly, they had loved him and supported him. After they had died, he hadn't felt the same, he had stopped going to his appointments, stopped meeting with friends. Stopped doing everything that had previously held any type of meaning for him. Idly Felix wondered if his parents would have been proud of him if they had still been around.

Felix couldn't imagine why they would.

Drumming up the courage to get on the bus was the most initiative Felix had managed to muster in years. If it didn't go well, it might well be the last time he bothered. The bus was getting close now, he could see the construction site that seemed to forever exist in a sort of paperwork limbo, originally it was going to be another grandiose hotel, one of many in the city. But the money had mysteriously dried up halfway through the project and it had been stuck as an unfinished mess ever since something for the people at the supermarket across the street to forever stare at in disgust.

The bus finally came to a stop and he stopped looking at the building and started to pay attention to the people. Thousands of them stood on the street, on the sidewalk, and tucked away in the shops that lined the main street of the city. Felix exited the bus, and he was immediately subsumed into the crowd, he was bumped back and forth for a while before he picked a direction and started walking which alleviated most of the collisions. The throngs of people almost held a tidal force and he felt himself being pulled along in their wake. Felix's heart thudded in his chest, but it wasn't in panic, but excitement. He wasn't afraid, Felix thought, but quickly realized he was walking in the wrong direction and twisted around, slipping into the flow of people going in the opposite direction.

The crowd despite its vastness was dwarfed in presence by the buildings on both sides of the street, tall multi-floor shopping complexes, hotels, and corporate buildings that scraped at the sky. The people in the street were starting to pull back away from the road in places all along the street and tried to join the people on the sidewalk and people were suddenly packed tight against the buildings.

Felix found himself stuck against one of the trees that sprung up out of the sidewalk every ten meters or so. The front of the march was in sight and the front line of people spanned the entire width of the road. They carried banners, flags, signs, giant hands, and a multitude of other objects. They cheered as they marched west down the street and the people on the sidewalk cheered and yelled in return.

Felix watched it in awe before he was abruptly struck in the side of the face with an elbow, which belonged to a man who was punching the air in his excitement. Felix turned to face away from him and found himself facing a young woman, roughly his age, who was pressed face-first against him, and Felix met her eyes.

She wore a brown coat and a beanie with two dangling baubles on her head, long brown hair streamed out and down her back. The woman looked remarkably at home with the situation with a grin on her face. A surge of panic welled up in his chest at the proximity and the eye contact, and Felix tried to step backward but he was stuck.

A young man, in the same age range, stood next to her, he was tall, muscular, and blonde. The blonde man was in much the same position and like Felix had his hand braced against the tree above the woman's head. Someone bumped him and he stumbled forward a step and he knocked Felix's hand from the tree. Felix flinched back from them and twisted around again to face the other direction, deliberately staring over the heads of people, and refusing to accidentally meet another pair of eyes.

Felix felt humiliation well up in him and couldn't believe that he had come here. This was a terrible idea, Felix thought miserably. He caught a flash of light in his peripheral vision and turned his head back towards the two people and looked over their heads. The light was gone, but abruptly there was another flash of light and his eyes snapped over to it in reflex.

There was a commotion in the throng of people before him, the crowd was opening before someone and closing behind them. Felix turned back around to try and identify what was happening behind them.

Whoever it was coming up the sidewalk and towards the tree they were pressed against, and quite quickly.

Further behind the moving obstruction he could see a bunch of the same gaps opening and closing, but he could see the torso and upper body of one exceedingly tall man, in a black suit and sunglasses pushing his way through the crowds in the same direction, there were no flashes of light in that group. A group of people chasing someone with a flashlight maybe.

Another flash of light, golden light, he noted, not a flashlight occurred between the tall man and Felix, but much closer now. His mind trying to connect the dots as someone yelled and fell backward after another golden flash.

What was happening?

Whoever it was, they were almost at the tree now, and a small feminine hand suddenly reached out and grabbed the blonde man on his forearm and with a flash of golden light, clearly being emitted from the palm of her hand. The blonde man started to collapse, but before he went all the way to the ground, he managed to grab the attacker's arm and wrenched it towards him. The blonde man collapsed backward into the tree and Felix reached out to steady him, but the man fell straight onto Felix in a heap, knocking them both to the ground.

The owner of the hand, with some detailed golden pattern on it, had fallen on top of them both. It was a woman with long black hair and pale white skin. She was wide eyed and frantic, she wore an extremely ruffled pantsuit, solid black. The woman in the beanie reached down to help the golden-hand woman up, and she took the offered hand with another flash of blinding golden light before the beanie girl went down in a heap as well.

Felix stared at the golden-hand woman as she pulled herself to her knees

and settled her frantic gaze on him. She reached out and Felix immediately kicked her in the face as hard as he could and tried to through
himself backward against the still yelling crowd, his shoe flew off and
the lady let out a cry of pain at the hit, but she kept on coming without
even a hint of hesitation and Felix had nowhere to go, so he fell back
on tried and true methods, attempting to kick her in the face again but
she blocked it easily with her palm. It felt like kicking a stone wall this
time and a burst of pain shot up his leg, her hand clenched around the
bottom of his foot, and with a flash of golden light, Felix knew no more.

Two

Felix woke up with his face was pressed flat against the floor, the material he was laying on was cold and unyielding. He opened his eyes slowly and with a moment's effort carefully pushed himself into a sitting position. The usual sense of sleepiness that lingered with him upon first waking up wasn't present, in its place was a wave of adrenaline that coursed through his body. He wiped at his eyes with the back of his hand and took in his surroundings, his heart thudding powerfully inside his chest.

What was this place? *Where* was this place?

The room he was in was large, and the floor was comprised of smooth squares of marble, which explained why it was so cold. Besides the fact that he had never seen this room before in his life the most pressing issue was that the room was *filled* with people. Some of them were still lying on the ground, hopefully unconscious, as Felix had been. Some of them were stirring, still in the process of waking up while the largest portion of the room's occupants was already awake and standing upright. There were groups of people talking to one another, while others were alone, sticking to the walls of the room and staring around suspiciously. One young woman was crying and holding her wrist, bent unnaturally, while an older man approached and sat down next to her, talking quietly.

Felix immediately became one of the quiet ones, standing up and moving to the nearest wall to observe everyone else in the room. Felix glanced down at his right foot; it still covered by his sock, but his shoe was nowhere in sight, the sole of his foot was tingling strangely, exactly where the pale woman had grabbed him, there was a brief moment where he considered investigating it but pushed the urge down for the moment. Felix stayed still and didn't bring any additional attention to himself, quietly kicking off his other shoe and sliding it across the floor away from him.

The room they were in had a single locked door, directly on the other side of the room from him, and it was large, made of some kind of dark metal. Felix knew It was locked because people were prying at it without any luck. He noted that the door had no handle at all, which was incredibly strange.

Felix wondered if he was a jail of some sort, before discarding the idea. Considering the events that had brought him here, it was most likely a *quarantine* of some kind. This probably wasn't a room in a hospital, judging by the expensive marble floors. Felix reached behind him surreptitiously and knocked on the wall, it was made of solid white material just as hard as the floor, completely normal. There was a series of modern circular lights inset into the ceiling, spaced evenly across the length of the room, settled flush with the rest of the ceiling. The sheer size of the room and the marble floors spoke of an expensive taste, but the fact that there was nothing inside it except for people was strange. It was a large building judging by the room, it reminded Felix of the aesthetic of the hotel he worked at, if slightly different in color.

It wasn't the basement of *his* hotel, of course, he had been in it before and it had been filled with machinery, pipes and other things. He looked at the other circles in the ceiling that weren't lighting; a series of speakers set into the roof like what he was used to at his hotel, a public address system; in case of an emergency. Four cameras; one in each corner of the room to give full coverage to whoever was watching.

Felix expected that they would be contacted through the speakers soon if they hadn't already while he was unconscious. No doubt whatever the gold-hand woman had infected them with required them to be kept away from others. Felix started studying the people trapped inside with him, there was no pattern he could discern from a casual glance, people of every race, sex, and class were represented and they had all dressed appropriately for the weather outside. There were quite a few people with clothing that had words painted on them, or in some case, their bodies, as one entirely topless woman had words painted across her chest. All these people had likely been present at the march, or at least nearby like Felix had been.

Some groups or individuals stood out even in such an eclectic crowd of people, like a tall man who was surrounded by a group of people, all of them vying for his attention. For being stuck in the middle of so many people he was looking remarkably composed, the man's body language was almost relaxed, he was used to such attention. Felix noted idly that the man was also one of the most handsome men he had ever seen in person, with sharp features and perfectly styled hair. He also looked vaguely familiar, but Felix couldn't quite place him. The people surrounding him were mostly women, the oldest of which looked to be in her thirties. Someone famous perhaps, from the internet? Perhaps a movie.

Felix looked elsewhere and found a person who bore a striking resemblance to the mayor of Saltwall City, there was something about his face was off, however, he also had a large group around him and was talking to a few of the older more business dressed occupants of the room.

Another standout was a man that had been moving between people since Felix woke up, shaking their hands and chatting happily and handing out business cards. He did not attempt to hide his actions, apparently at ease with talking to people he had possibly never met before. Why he had so many of the cards on him was entirely up for de-bate, but he was making sure to canvas everyone in an exhaustive pattern that took him to the wall, and back the other way, he would be at Felix's position in ten minutes or so.

Perhaps the most interesting person in the room was the short woman standing only a few meters away who wore a hooded sweatshirt and was somehow radiating a sickening sense of dread. Felix couldn't understand why everyone else was standing so close to the woman, let alone how they seemingly didn't notice the intense feeling. She had her hand over her mouth, muffling the small noises she was making, while her eyes were wide and excited as they jumped around the room. Her shoulders trembled now and then, and she was visibly trying to reign in some sort of manic energy.

When the woman glanced at Felix he immediately turned away and looked somewhere else. Felix had never seen body language in a combination like that before, but he could put together the individual signs well enough. The woman was excited, eager, and gleeful, for some reason she was happy to be in this room. Had she wanted to come here, was she in league with the woman with the gold light? What was this sickening feeling that was pressing down on him? How was she even doing it?

A flash of blonde in the corner of Felix's eye drew his attention, and his eyes flickered over to it. It was the muscular blonde man from the tree and he was walking in his direction, *directly* at him. The man's eyes were locked onto his and Felix found he couldn't look away, the horrible dread that the short woman was emitting seemed to temper his anxiety somehow how strange, his mind felt sharper then it had in a long time.

The blonde guy stopped next to him and clapped his hand on Felix's shoulder with a smile.

"Hey! You were there when I got dropped." He said cheerfully.

Felix nodded at him, but his attention was completely on the man's arm where a golden leaf of some kind was visible. The leaf was exactly where the pale woman had grabbed him earlier. Felix distinctly remembered that the man's arm had been completely bare earlier, this mark was new. Felix thought of his still tingling foot as he stared at the mark without comprehension, it was pulsing gently as if it were filled with strange energy;

Felix had never seen anything like it. The guy had realized that he had lost Felix's attention for the moment because he followed his gaze down to his arm and the mark.

"Yeah! This thing!" The man said sounding surprised, before moving his arm close so that Felix could see it more clearly.

"No idea what the hell it even is," He continued and frowned at his arm like it had displeased him somehow.

Felix found it somehow easy to speak to the man while that sickening feeling of dread overwhelmed him.

"How is it glowing like that?" Felix asked quietly, without any accompanying anxiety.

The man glanced at Felix and then back down at the mark and his frown deepened.

"I don't know," The man said simply, "Kind of freaky to be honest."

Freaky? Felix thought it wasn't really, but it *was* strange.

How was the leaf glowing though? Had someone placed a light source under his skin somehow; Felix had seen people on the internet who had placed objects beneath their skin. If they peeled back the skin would there be a strip of LED lights beneath the mark? Felix did a quick scan of the room looking at people's bodies, but nobody else had a visible mark like it. Felix looked down at his foot again which was still tingling, he hesitated thinking of reaching down to check but stopped himself.

Felix looked back at the blond guy to find that he was watching the short woman with a frown and waiting patiently for him to respond. Felix almost asked him if he also felt it, but it was obvious that he did so he didn't bother.

"It's in the same place the woman grabbed you." Felix said quietly, and after a moment continued, "I can't see anyone else with a visible mark."

The blond man grabbed his chin and nodded thoughtfully.

"Yeah, same spot and everything. It was a woman that got me? I didn't see who it was, I just felt them grab my arm."

Felix remembered abruptly that the guy had immediately reacted, trying to drag the person into a grapple; the guy's reflexes were nothing to scoff at.

"Do you do martial arts?" Felix asked curiously, already knowing the answer.

The man's eyes lit up and he nodded again.

"Yeah! How did you know?" The man asked happily.

Besides the bulging muscle? Felix didn't say.

"You tried to grab the person as soon as that golden light went off," Felix said easily.

The man grinned at Felix.

"I'm Charles, what's your name?" Charles asked him cheerfully and stuck out his hand for him to shake.

"Felix," Felix replied easily and took it without hesitation.

Felix was marveling at having a normal conversation for once, his anxiety completely gone, but the PA system abruptly turned on and dragged him out of his thoughts. For a moment the awful sound of feedback cut through the room before a woman's voice came through the speakers loud and clear.

"Good afternoon, everybody. Please remain calm." The female voice said calmly.

Some people started yelling and cursing the voice, but the PA system didn't respond to any of it. People eventually fell into an uneasy silence after almost five minutes had passed and then the woman spoke again.

"Please remain calm, is there anybody who currently has a glowing symbol shaped like a leaf present somewhere on their body? If so, please approach the door. I will ask everybody else to step away from the door, you are in danger." The female voice said calmly.

Felix was already looking back at Charles when she had mentioned the mark. Felix's first thought was that the way she had implied it was 'dangerous' was strange. Was the mark infectious? Did it seem unlikely with such a perfect tattoo like shape, that had to be by design how was a strip of golden light dangerous? But the voice was asking if *anyone* had the mark, which indicated that they hadn't known who *had* it and who *didn't*. Charles met his gaze for a moment and nodded, before taking a step in the direction of the door. Felix forced himself to speak before he was out of range.

"Hey Charles, be careful. We don't know who these people are, or what they want. They might try to hurt you or something." Charles looked surprised at the thought and nodded at him again before turning away.

Charles visibly steeled himself before stepping forward and announcing his presence in a loud voice.

"Glowing arm man, coming through!" Charles said with a laugh.

Despite the absurdity of the remark, everyone stepped back out of his path like he had the plague. Felix couldn't understand how Charles could be so confident in the face of so much focused attention, every single person in the room was staring at him.

Surprisingly, when Charles reached the door another person stepped out of the crowd as well and walked up beside him. It was a short woman, five foot even on her best day with long auburn hair. She wore an oversized woolly sweater and a pleated skirt. On her bare left leg was a golden glowing leaf, the same shape, and size as Charles's own.

Felix's mind raced at that; it couldn't possibly be some kind of infection, it was silly to think that it would result in two perfectly symmetrical glowing marks, these had to be deliberately placed there.

The woman on the PA system repeated her warning of danger and then opened the door, revealing several men in black suits with black sunglasses covering there faces, all standing calmly in the hallway beyond.

Everybody had moved far back at this point and away from the two at the door, probably thinking that the danger present was the marks on their skin despite the woman not clarifying. The sight of the golden marks, it had made the situation real to all of them; evidence that something very abnormal was going on.

Charles and the woman with auburn-hair stepped out of the room and the doors shut quickly behind them leaving us in the room once more. Everybody else waited for something to happen, but almost ten minutes had passed before the PA system crackled back to life.

"Please form orderly lines, you will be leaving one at a time. If anyone attempts to leave the room out of turn, the doors will be locked for six hours." The female voice said calmly.

People complained, but nobody was going to be the one responsible for getting them all locked up for an additional six hours, so they complied and immediately started to form a rough line in front of the door.

The somewhat orderly line made it easier for Felix to count them, and he did so while remaining right at the back of the room. He counted three times and got different results each time, people moving around or some who were hidden behind others made it difficult to get a perfect number from his position.

There was somewhere between ninety-six and one-hundred and seven people. Not including those who had left the room already, Felix stayed against the wall and watched the line move slowly over the next two hours. The woman emitting the dread aura had joined the very back of the line, and as she moved closer to the doors and further away from Felix he felt the dread slowly recede. There was a pattern to it all, the door would open, someone would step out, and the door would close again, somewhere between five to ten minutes would pass before the door would open again. There was still something wrong with all of this.

What could he glean from this?

One person through the door at a time, it worked to keep the people outside of the room isolated and easy to handle. Nothing was being communicated back to anyone in the room, which could mean that anything could be going on outside and the remaining people wouldn't know until it was too late. If this was a normal crisis with police oversight or even some kind of military intervention, constant communication would be used to keep tempers low and defuse the situation.

This was not the case in the room, the PA system had not spoken again other than to warn them to back away from the door when the front of the line had gotten too close. Two separate fights had already broken out during the waiting and both ended with bloodied faces and other people dragging the combatants away from each other. The woman on the PA system didn't say anything, didn't tell them not to fight, didn't try to keep them calm; nothing. Felix frowned; they were being watched the cameras were in the four corners of the room, but whoever as watching didn't care if anyone was injured in some way, that was extremely unusual.

Felix switched gears abruptly to avoid his thoughts hitting a dead end.

A single person had touched them to place the marks, and other people in black suits were chasing *her*. Some people got the mark, while others didn't; some quality that Charles and the auburn-haired woman had possessed. Felix glanced again at his right foot, some quality that he may possess as well.

Their captors didn't care if they hurt each other, and when they asked for those with the mark to approach the doors, they had also told them that anyone who tried to leave would be in danger. But they didn't say by *who*, it wasn't the marked people, they had both been regular people and Charles seemed like a decent person. Charles and the short woman with auburn hair had been in here with us the entire time without *any* issues.

It hadn't been a warning for the safety of those still in the room, it had been a *threat*.

A feeling of rising dread started to build up that had nothing to do with the woman at the back of the line. What were they doing to the people on the other side of the door? The line was shorter now, and Felix approached slowly, staying well clear of the people near the back. He was close enough that he could hear some of the people talking and even make out the words.

Felix noticed that the tall, handsome man, who Felix had assumed was a celebrity, was still chatting happily with some of his fans. They were exchanging stories of where the woman had 'tasered' them. One woman was fussing over the celebrity's face, but he waved her off laughing, saying it hadn't even left a mark. Felix held back a snort, although the thought of getting shocked in the face by a taser was unpleasant, the idea that it had been a taser in the first place was *ridiculous*.

The other man that had been doing the canvasing earlier approached Felix, who was still standing a large distance away from the back of the line. Felix found himself hyper-focused on the man immediately and almost turned away from the man before he managed to stop himself. Instead, he just stood still and waited, embarrassed.

"Nice to meet you!" The man said and stuck out his hand to shake. "I'm Shane."

Felix forced himself to take Shane's hand to avoid the awful silence that would follow if he didn't.

"Felix," Felix mumbled.

Shane flicked a business card out of his front pocket and held it out to him. Felix took it careful not to touch the other man's fingers before glancing down at it. 'Shane's used cars!' was printed along the top in blue letters while the contact and address details were below it in smaller font. Shane continued after a moment, seemingly unaware of his awkwardness.

"You should drop by after all this," Shane said easily while waving his hand at the other people in the room and then the door.

Felix opened his mouth to tell him that he didn't need a car, but Shane cut him off.

"Not for a car! Just to talk about this craziness. We should group up, *all* of us," Shane stressed the word.

He was not talking about just the two of them, but everyone who had been inside the room, Felix nodded without commitment and dropped his gaze to the man's nose to avoid eye contact.

"Whatever this was, it was handled so poorly; we should be able to sue *someone*. It's would be an easy win even, open and shut, *probably*." Shane rattled off, not giving him a chance to respond.

Which was fine by Felix, he just started to nod along after that, so that Shane might leave him alone sooner. Shane abruptly changed topics and asked Felix where they'd 'gotten him', having overheard the continuing conversation in front of us,

"Shoulder." Felix lied and awkwardly touched himself on the left shoulder.

"They got *me* on the hand," Shane nodded and pointed to his left hand, as close as he was, Felix thought he could see a faint yellow discoloration.

The conversation trailed off quickly after that and Shane re-joined the line with another request to come to see him 'after'. A little while later the famous guy waved to his fans and walked calmly through the door with a smile on his face.

Felix was still feeling worried, however, and the muffled giggles of the dread-woman weren't helping his nerves. She was the last person in line, and she kept looking back at Felix with wild eyes. Felix decided that he wasn't going anywhere near her again; she could leave first because Felix was determined on going last.

Another couple of people left, and it was then Shane's turn. He gave them both a wave as he stepped through the door and received a giggle in return, seemingly not at all wary of the giggling thing. Which just left Felix and the giggling thing behind. The tension started to ratchet up with every passing second. The feeling of dread was getting stronger too, almost like it was uncoiling, what was wrong with this woman? Was it even a person? What was it doing?

Felix stared at the back of its head, and it just kept giggling. Abruptly she turned around and stared at him, and he couldn't bring himself to look away. She removed her hand from her face for the first time since entering the room and there was something wrong with her face, she looked like a woman, young, maybe twenty, but her mouth was far too wide, reaching almost to the sides of her face and her lips were peeled back in a massive grin, showing all her teeth, of which there were far too many.

"Don't you want to get out of here?" The thing asked, still giggling.

It looked like a person, but the proportions of every feature were off slightly, it wasn't ugly but it looked unnatural. Felix didn't feel the anxiousness he usually felt whenever someone focused their attention on him. Just an unending feeling of dread, like if he took his eyes off it for a single second he would die.

Felix stared at it unblinking.

"You're not human, why were you in here with us?" Felix asked it quietly.

The thing pretending to be a woman giggled again.

"Nobody else noticed! Not even the Collectors!" The thing said gleefully before it descended into peals of laughter as if it was the funniest thing in the world.

It might well have been, but Felix lacked the context to appreciate the humor. The thing took a step towards Felix and he immediately stepped backward an equal distance.

The door opened suddenly and the thing stopped advancing on him, seemingly conflicted. Felix could see the group of people in black suits still standing just outside the door watching them. The thing brought its hand up and chewed on its thumb for a moment before giggling again.

"Lucky, Lucky!" It said and turned and walked through the door.

The doors started to swing shut before someone fell between them, leaving the left side of the door partially open, but Felix didn't move from his spot. When ten minutes had finally passed and the screaming had finally stopped, Felix walked out of the still open doors and into the hallway making sure to avoid the bodies on the floor.

Felix turned to his left and found a long hallway, there were doors spaced regularly down the length of it, on both sides of the walkway. The walls were streaked red with blood, and the floor was littered with the body parts of the people who had held them captive, Felix just stared up the hallway for a long time unable to bring himself to cross the distance. The bodies were well dressed, the men wore black suits and the women wore pantsuits of the same color, some had sunglasses on. The same people who had been waiting outside in the hallway.

Nothing moved in the hallway except the rising and falling of his chest, and it took a few, minutes before his heart's frantic attempt at escaping his chest finally slowed. Felix noted that every single person was missing some part of their body or had a chunk of flesh missing. The man closest to him didn't even *have* a left leg anymore, and the closest woman was missing a large section of her shoulder, the arm dangled by a tenacious thread of flesh.

Felix pulled his shirt up to his mouth and took a deep breath through it, before slowly walking forward down the hall, picking his way through the bodies, finding empty spaces for his feet to avoiding slipping on all the blood, pausing for a moment once he had reached the first door on his left, which was still partially open.

Felix reached out and nudged it the rest of the way open with his foot and glanced inside. Shane was sitting in the only chair in the room, his left arm was strapped to the table in front of him by the forearm, but the hand was missing entirely. The man who was likely responsible was in the corner of the room with a large meat cleaver stuck in his head. A section of his black suit was torn, and a massive chunk of his left pectoral muscle was missing from his chest. They were both dead, so Felix turned and left the room without a word. He walked to the staircase at the end of the hall and he didn't stop to check any more of the doors.

The stairs twisted up and to the left out of sight, and he climbed them silently, feeling numb and detached from everything around him, he crested the staircase and stepped into the lobby of a hotel; but it wasn't familiar at all. There were even more bodies in the lobby, and they were all wearing black suits and missing body parts.

People walked past the glass frontage of the building without taking any notice of what had happened inside. Those who looked at the build went glassy-eyed briefly and continued unaware of what had recently occurred. Felix walked to the front of the building and out of the doors, onto the sidewalk. Felix knew where he was in an instant, he was right across the road from the bus stop he had gotten off earlier.

A lady in an expensive-looking coat was sitting outside of the supermarket staring at her phone, it was angled in his direction. He turned and looked up at the building he had just exited, and Felix knew without a shadow of a doubt that in this exact spot had been an empty construction sight only hours before. The words 'Otherside' was written above the glass frontage and he turned away after a moment.

Felix didn't stop and wait for the bus; he turned left and didn't stop walking until he was home.

Felix sat on the floor of his shower staring at the sole of his right foot. It was gently pulsing with a golden glow, and his foot tingled in time with every pulse. It was shaped like a leaf, with thicker golden lines running down the center and branching off on either side. It grew bright when he touched it and faded slightly when he stopped. He poked and prodded it and watched the brightness wax and wane for hours.

Whenever his thoughts drifted towards the hotel, he shut down the line of thought immediately, only able to bring himself to move once the water started to run cold, and he began to shiver. He dried himself off with a fluffy white towel, appropriated from his workplace, and left it hanging on a hook in the bathroom before walking to his bed naked. He sat on the bed and lifted his leg and place his foot into his lap.

What did this thing do exactly? It had to be something important.

The people from the Otherside had removed the only people with visible marks right at the beginning, were Charles and the short lady dead? Had they killed them first because they were more valuable or were they special in some way and they did something else with them. If he had taken his sock off back in the room and proclaimed that he was 'glowing footman' would he be dead right now?

The thing that had been in the room with him; it had eaten parts of every single person in the building. Did those people also have these marks? The men in the black suits had cut of Shane's hand and then had been killed before they could do much more. Shane had bled out while stuck to the table, but where were all the other people from the room? Had they disposed of them already somehow, there were around a hundred people at the start, and that had to be far too many missing people in a single day to just cover up, surely.

The families and friends, their employer's and employees and everyone else that were in their lives would notice if they had suddenly disappeared. Felix could hear police sirens in the distance, and for several very long minutes, he thought that they had noticed and were coming to pick him up. But instead, the sirens simply continued past his apartment without any fuss, it took him a long minute to calm down.

Felix took a deep breath, nobody was looking for him, people couldn't even see the hotel, nobody knew it was there. It had been invisible to him this morning, and visible to him now; the only thing of note that had changed was the mark. So, there was one thing that was confirmed to do, it enabled you to see invisible things.

Hidden buildings in the middle of a city, there *had* to be others.

Was every construction site in the city a front? If it was, that meant an entire society of people were hidden in plain sight, Felix doubted that turning a building invisible was the only thing they could do. What about people, he had been able to see the man in the black suit before he had been marked, but could they make *people* invisible?

He looked down at his foot and focused his mind.

"Turn invisible, foot," Felix demanded.

His foot stubbornly remained where it was and refused to vanish, and he sighed before dropping it to the floor, his knee hurt from holding the position for so long anyway. He did his best to refocus his thoughts in a more helpful direction, which was the next most important thing?

The thing in the room, it had somehow killed an entire building full of people. Some of the people in the suits had been approaching seven-foot, like that one guy in the crowd this morning. The thing had to of been stronger than a normal human to fight its way through that many people.

Did it have one of these marks?

It had been wearing a hoody and jeans, the only skin you could see was the hands and the face. It had looked like a human, but it hadn't acted like one. All the bodies had been missing things, and the only clean-cut had been Shane's arm curtesy of the cleaver. Everything else had been torn, ripped off, or chewed which meant that the thing was probably *eating* the marks.

It had called them the 'Collectors', and they had to have been cutting off the marks for some reason, collecting them if you went by the name. The marks might have been a source of food for the thing, but what benefit did they provide the Collectors? The giggling thing and the collectors were on opposite sides and in a conflict of some sort. It had been amused that they hadn't noticed that it had slipped in with the dozens of unconscious bodies.

It wasn't just strong, it was also cunning, the worst kind of combination for a monster to possess.

There might even be more of them or other places like the Otherside filled with more of the Collectors. Felix knew that almost all of this was just speculation; he could only know for sure what he had seen and try and drawn a realistic conclusion from that data.

What he needed was to find some *more* data, something that would allow him to build a better idea of what was going on, fill out the picture a little more to allow him to make decisions on what he should do. Felix needed to figure out if someone was going to come after him for what had happened at that hotel, or if the thing was going to get hungry and come find him for dinner.

The thing Felix needed *most* of all; was to sleep.

Three

When Felix woke up the golden mark was still on his foot and he hadn't been assaulted or eaten in the middle of the night. He spent almost an hour poking at the mark on his foot and trying to get it to do something, eventually, he was just poking it to watch it change. Why did it get brighter, and why did it fade? It was like it was trying to do *something*, but Felix didn't know what the next step was.

He eventually got up and got dressed, slowly making his way through his daily routine almost entirely on autopilot, while trying to think up a plan of action for the day. He needed to figure out what he was going to do about everything that had happened.

Should he go to the police? Post something anonymously online? What if they couldn't see the building? What if they knew about it already, and allowed it to happen? What if that group worked with the police in the first place? The only thing that had occurred to him so far; was to go back to the Otherside. This was not the best idea ever for obvious reasons; it was full of dead bodies for one and was also the last known location of the monstrous thing that had killed and eaten them all.

It had occurred to Felix while tossing and turning in bed that the Otherside was a *hotel*, which meant that it catered to *guests*, guests who could see the building. Any of the guests that had been out, or had come looking to rent a room might have returned in the meantime. Which meant that they were probably looking for the parties involved in the mess. Felix was one of those parties, for better or for worse but, it was also the only method he knew, to get additional information about the strange situation.

Felix flicked on the news to use as background noise and made some breakfast.

There was nothing on the news about any major disappearances which made absolutely no sense whatsoever, over a *hundred* people had vanished yesterday, and nobody was saying a damn thing about it, there *had* to be camera footage of the march, or people that saw the unconscious people being dragged away; it was insane.

There *was* a short segment about some actor that had been found dead in his apartment earlier this morning but nobody knew any details about his death yet, but they put up a picture of his face to accompany the news presenter's report. It was the guy from the room, that had been 'tasered' in the face. Felix glanced down at the name scrolling past, Kaiden Sharp, an actor found dead in his apartment.

The Collectors had moved him, sometime before the thing had killed everyone, they might have returned soon after he'd left the building, only to find everybody in Otherside dead, or if they were exceedingly fast, they might have returned just in time to be killed by the thing as well.

This was the next piece of the puzzle, what could he extrapolate from this?

There were no News reports about a hundred *non-famous* people being found dead in their apartments, so what had happened to everyone else? Did they send all the others back to their homes missing limbs or sections of their bodies? Wouldn't the injured say something? Or their family members?

Felix was guessing that Kaiden's mark would have been on his face had it appeared. Felix, Charles, and the auburn-haired woman all had a visible mark, and he could confirm that at least two of those three had the marks located where they had been touched. Felix imagined it would be hard to remove someone's face without killing them.

Did the Collectors just say to hell with it?

Felix needed to find someone from the room, someone that was still alive. That would be his primary goal, eventually, someone would discover the Otherside situation and try to clean up any loose ends. Felix could go to Shane's workplace in a couple of weeks and ask about his whereabouts. He should be able to learn something from their response if they spun some story to his family and friends it might give him another lead. If they didn't say anything at all to them, it would still reveal some information about how they acted. That didn't help him *now* though, and they might just bury Shane's body somewhere and never try and cover anything up at all.

More than anything Felix wanted to just ignore it all and get on with doing nothing for the rest of his miserable life but he couldn't, he was in danger even if he didn't know exactly what form it would take. There was a hidden society tucked away in Saltwall City that had existed for god knows how long, and the people that were in it were running around cutting off people's limbs to get to the golden marks.

There were monstrous things that looked like people that could kill at least a hundred people twice its size in a couple of minutes, and it was *eating* the marks off people as well. Felix had a golden mark of his own, eventually, someone was going to either cut it off or eat it *neither* of which sounded like fun. He needed to keep ahead of this, or he was going to end up dead anyway.

Going back to the Hotel would be option number two for now, even if it ended up with him being killed slightly earlier then if he did nothing but hiding. Option number one was something he could find out about right now; he went down the stairs of his apartment building and onto the small green courtyard that sat alongside the road in front of the building.

He stopped in front of the sign that was staked into the ground, it had a large smiling face on the front, the mayor; his re-election campaign had begun a couple of weeks ago. Felix stared at it and tried to match the features from the sign with the man from the room. They weren't the same person, but they were very similar. Too old to be the mayor's son, it was instead most likely his brother. This was a solid lead; Felix needed to go and find the Mayor's brother, too see if he was missing anything important.

Felix had his goals, now he just had to make them a reality.

He returned to his room and did a cursory google search which revealed that the Mayor's brother was called, Eric Stately. He wasn't a part of the government, or even the city council like Felix had assumed, but instead, it turned out that Eric was the CEO of a multinational pharmaceutical company. It brought with it the question of why such a man had been at the march in the first place.

It wasn't as important everything else going on, so he dropped it.

What he needed now was to figure out how he could engineer a situation where he could physically see Eric or at least his current condition. Felix thought he could sit outside the man's workplace and wait for him to appear, but it didn't seem like the best use of his time. The man probably wouldn't be at work on a Sunday, and Felix didn't have any idea when he would be or even where the building was. He instead tried to look up whether Eric was a public speaker of some kind, or if he participated in any public events in the past or planned to soon, that would require Eric to show up physically to an event.

Felix would be able to check if he was missing anything important under those conditions, instead of anything he was actively looking for the first thing Felix found was a News story, posted exactly three minutes ago. It was a video of the man exiting his house with his wife and children, a giant of a man dressed in a black suit escorted him to his car, the reporter asked after his health.

Eric stopped and gave the reporter a small conversation.

The first thing Felix noted was that Eric's left arm was missing, the end of it was covered in bandages. There was no way he should be walking around merely hours after having it cut off, Felix wasn't buying it. The Collectors had to have been able to heal or close the wound somehow. Erik told a brief story about a malignant tumor and the unfortunate event of having to get his arm amputated. Eric laughed at something the reporter had said and told her it wouldn't keep him down for long. He looked like he was telling the truth, he made ample eye contact with the reporter and answered her questions pleasantly, his body language was open, and he didn't appear to be in any pain.

It made no sense, they had abducted a man, cut off his arm, returned him to his home in the middle of the night and everyone was none the wiser. His family wasn't alarmed, Eric didn't seem alarmed but Felix certainly *felt* alarmed.

How did they accomplish that?

They had to of messed with the man's memory, but how many people in Eric's life had seen the man with both arms before yesterday? How would they go about dealing with those people? It didn't escape his notice that Eric hadn't mentioned anything about the room. Did they mess with the memory of every single person that had been abducted? Returned them to their homes with tales of tumors, car accidents, and bear attacks?

These collector people were terrifying, and if there was any left after what that monster had done to them they likely wanted to cut off Felix's foot, he needed to check the hotel as soon as possible and he needed to know *what* they were doing all of this for, he needed to find out *how* they were doing it and he needed to know how he could protect *himself* from them.

Felix spent hours brainstorming everything and anything he could think of, but he kept circling back to just going to the hotel. It was the only thing he could think of doing and when the clock finally struck the tenth hour Felix stood up and left his apartment. Felix took the same bus he had the day before, sat in the same seat even, and looked out of the same window. It unnerved him, almost like a repeat of the day before, but will fewer people be wandering the streets. The bus driver was a different man as well, which made him feel slightly better.

He stared out the window, trying to look at everything at once, scanning the city for buildings that hadn't existed yesterday. Buildings that had suddenly sprung into existence where empty lots and construction sites used to be but he couldn't find anything on the route, but something in the distant skyline *had* changed and Felix focused on it with a sense of unease, but he couldn't tell exactly which building it was, and it sent a pang of alarm through him. He tried to dig up a memory of looking at that same view before, there was something just out of reach that he couldn't remember. Was it the building towards the left side of the city with dark blue glass?

He wasn't sure, and it frightened him.

It was out of sight a second later and he didn't manage to reacquire the angle needed to see it again, the building surrounding him were far too tall to him to see it, he would have to look again on the way back. Felix was faintly worried that he would start seeing new buildings everywhere, jumping at every shadow only to find that it had been there all along.

He would have to search for the city through with a map on his phone, starting with Otherside. If the Otherside failed to show up on the map he could go through the city on the block by block and note any suspicious building. He would be able to then walk past or even enter some of the building if they were stores and check if anything funny was going on, it wasn't the most efficient thing he had ever thought of but it was the best he could come up with.

They rounded the corner and the Otherside finally came into view on the street before the bus came to a stop at the same bus spot as yesterday. Felix climbed out and immediately started walking back up the street and away from the building, heading for a cafe with a spread of chairs both inside and out. 'Bust a bean!' was written proudly across the frontage in blocky blue letters.

Felix entered the café and headed straight for the queue at the counter, which was moving quickly. Felix wondered how busy it would become during the lunch rush with a tinge of uncertainty. When he reached the front of the line, he mumbled out his order, and the barista noted it down, before cheerfully telling him to take a seat and they would bring it out.

Felix mumbled a thank you and wandered to a seat near the corner of the room that had an unobstructed view of the Otherside, through the glass doors on the side of the café. Felix sat quietly and watched the building, parked in the drop off zone Infront of the hotel there was a black van that sparkled and gleamed in the light. Felix noted the number plate down in his phone, he had no idea what he could do with it, but if he ended up forwarding anything to the police, he could include the number plate. If he ever spotted another black van in the vicinity of the building he could check if the number matched, if he came here regularly and found more vehicles, he might be able to figure out a general number of cars and people that the Collectors had access too, it would take months but it was *something*.

The barista brought out his coffee after a moment and he mumbled out another thank you. Felix sat there for several hours and watched the many people come and go from the café, but nobody ever came out of or entered the Otherside. Eventually, Felix began to feel a strange feeling come over him, and it wasn't until it had solidified into a very faint sense of dread that he realized he was in danger.

Felix searched the room and quickly spotted the cause, but it was just a normal woman, drinking by herself quietly with a book in her hand. Now and then she would glance up in his direction before looking back to her book. It made him incredibly uncomfortable when he noted that her feet were pointed directly at him. The woman's posture was relaxed though, and she seemed completely at ease in the noisy café, with one of her arms was hidden beneath the table out of view.

Occasionally her eyes would flicker about the room for a moment, taking in the surroundings and any new customers that had appeared before returning to her book. Felix had realized immediately that she was watching him, which probably meant that she was one of the Collectors. The woman placed the book down on the table to brush a lock of black hair out of her eyes before lifting her cup to her mouth with the same hand.

Felix tensed minutely as he realized that this was the woman who had been sitting in front of the supermarket yesterday with her phone pointed in his direction. The lady immediately glanced up at his slight movement and her gaze became razor sharp. Felix forced himself to relax back into his chair and take a moment to let the panic wash out of him.

She couldn't get to him while he was in the cafe, there were far too many people here for that, Felix would have time to plan his escape, he was safe for now. He decided to see if he could spook her into leaving, so he stood up abruptly and walked straight in her direction, she glanced up in shock and dropped her book, but he turned when he rounded a table about halfway across the room and approached the counter instead too ordered another coffee.

He returned to his seat afterward to keep an eye on the woman, but she hadn't picked her book back up, instead, she was just staring straight at him without bothering to keep up appearances anymore, her hair had fallen into her eyes and she flicked it over her shoulder before standing up herself.

Felix watched as she stepped around the table and headed towards him slowly and spent the next few moments mentally eviscerating himself for provoking the woman like an idiot. He pulled his phone out of his pocket and pretended to use it as if his dismissal of her presence might make her go away.

The rising sense of dread became clearer as she got closer, but it wasn't anything like the thing in the room, barely a hundredth of the strength, if that. The sense of dread continued to rise with every step she took, and the woman's attention settled on Felix like a weight on his shoulders. The woman stopped right in front of his table, he awkwardly looked at her and immediately noticed her right arm was missing from the elbow down. He looked up met her gaze, his anxiety once again strangely absent and she smiled brightly at him.

"Hi, mind if I sit down?" She asked pleasantly.

Felix didn't believe the facade for a second, but he nodded anyway, and the woman sat down, not across from him as he expected, but directly adjacent to him on the bench seat. Felix moved so they weren't touching legs anymore, and she raised an eyebrow at him, but he ignored it.

"Wow, it's much easier to watch the building from over here." She said looking out the side door.

Felix stared at her, surprised she would just break her cover.

"It was getting annoying watching from the mirror." She continued after a moment.

The mirror was above and to the left of him, Felix had noted that it had shown a good angle of the building when he had first come in, but his seat was the better option long-term though so he had discarded it.

"Watching the Otherside?" Felix said easily.

He needed answers and this woman clearly knew something about the situation, and the faint sense of dread had temporarily trumped his anxiety allowing him to speak freely.

"I thought you were watching me until I remembered the mirror," Felix said idly.

The woman turned towards him and Felix leaned a little bit further away, it gave him a better look at her posture.

"Interesting that you can see the place at all." She said bemused, "Even stranger that you just strolled out of there yesterday with no shoes.'

The woman watched him, fishing for a reaction and Felix was hyper-focused on her reaction in turn.

"It wasn't cheap, it almost cost me an arm and a leg," Felix said carelessly.

The woman's shoulder twitched, her eyebrows narrowed, and her mouth tensed in contempt before it was all washed away an instant later.

"Seems like you have a similar experience with their high prices." Felix continued easily, astounded that he hadn't stuttered.

The woman watched him for a long moment before her lip twitched up at the corner.

"Let's not be hyperbolic, it's not quite as expensive as you said," She took a sip of her coffee before she continued, "It only cost me an arm."

She was smiling despite the horrifying undertones to the conversation and Felix nodded, once before they fell into a silence when the barista brought over his coffee, the two women made some small talk, but Felix just watched and didn't participate.

The two women chatted together like they were old friends; Felix could never do that with a stranger, he thought bitterly, ignoring the abnormal conversation he was having right now. Perhaps he could harness this dread-woman to cure his anxiety, the thought was absurd but amusing. The interruption was useful however and it gave Felix a moment to get his thoughts in order.

This woman, whose name he needed to get very soon, had probably been taken to the Otherside, they had removed her arm and let her go. Somehow, she still had her memories of the event, unlike what he had assumed with the Mayor's brother. This seemed to be contradictory to every conclusion he had come to. Did this mean he was wrong about Eric Stately? Was he faking the memory loss or maybe he was being blackmailed?

Either way, this woman had been watching the Otherside for an undisclosed period, likely much longer than he had been. So, she probably wasn't one of the people from the room *yesterday*, she had to of been in a previous batch that had been taken. He should ask how long ago, to get an idea of the frequency of when the Collectors took people. This suggested a glaring hole he had somehow missed, the woman that had run from the collectors, and given out marks during the march was not a regular event. Was this a much greater intake of people than normal? Did the collectors usually only capture one or two people?

Felix didn't know.

The other glaring question was why would a woman that had something so horrific happen to her, be so willing to stay near the building that it had happened in? There was another problem, her mark was gone along with her arm, yet she could still see the building somehow. Did that mean that once you had been marked there was no going back?

If the veil hiding the building from view only went one way, why hadn't anyone re-noticed the buildings that had sprung up across the city then? If Eric stately *did* have his memory erased and he took a stroll through the city wouldn't he suddenly be able to see a bunch of new buildings? Wouldn't he try and figure out where they had come from or would they just erase him memory again?

Felix shook his head.

These were all questions for later when he wasn't sitting next to a potential enemy. What was important right now, was that this woman wanted *something*, revenge, or otherwise. When the barista left the two of them alone with a wink, Felix tore his gaze away from her in embarrassment. He found the woman looking at him in amusement, Felix frowned at her.

"What is your name? I can't keep thinking of you as 'the woman' in my head." Felix said quietly and she raised an eyebrow at him.

"Oh? Do I spend a lot of time in your head?" She grinned, and Felix forced himself to roll his eyes, but he still felt his cheeks heat up.

He kept watching her in silence until she realized that he wasn't going to respond until she answered.

"Naomi," Naomi said pleasantly, breaking the stalemate with a pleasant smile. "and you are?"

Felix wasn't sure giving her his name was a good idea, there was a chance that she was lying about everything and that she *was* a Collector, but if she was going to murder him anyway, it would likely be a moot point.

"Felix," Felix answered quietly, after a moment.

It *probably* wasn't a good idea to provoke her again, what with the palpable aura of dread she had wafting off her, but the same reasoning applied as before, it didn't matter if Naomi was going to murder him anyway,

"Trying to get a refund?" Felix asked curiously, refereeing to her arm.

Naomi nodded, seemingly unperturbed at the comment, and didn't even try to deny it.

"Something like that, it's not quite as easy as one might imagine." Naomi smiled suddenly, showing off her perfect white teeth. "Their customer service needs some work."

Felix felt a flicker of amusement before he smothered it, Naomi tilted her head, allowing her hair to fall in front of her eyes.

"What about you? No missing pieces that I can see," Naomi grinned like a shark, before glancing down pointedly at his lap. 'Unless?'

Felix flushed, leaning back away from her and crossing his arms.

"Hilarious, I managed to leave on my terms thanks, unmolested," Felix said acidly but winced when the poor word choice hit him a moment.

Naomi just laughed.

"I've never seen someone so new to all of this escape the Collectors intact," Naomi said honestly and settled back into her chair. "The Otherside has been a ghost town since yesterday. Mind filling me in on what happened?"

Felix was going to bargain obviously; he wasn't just going to give her the information for free. He quickly decided on what was most important to him right then and discarded everything else, he was already flagging between the dread-aura and having a full-blown conversation with someone for the first time in years, and it was draining him fast.

"Tell you what, Naomi," Felix said plainly, forcing himself to say her name. "Tell me everything you know about the mark, and I'll tell you everything I know about what happened yesterday at the Otherside."

Naomi was quiet for a long moment, no doubt putting together that Felix knew absolutely nothing about this crazy hidden society by the trade offer, he'd very likely given the game away, if Naomi was working for Otherside this would be about the time his usefulness started to decline rapidly, and as soon as he told her what she wanted to know, he'd be up shit creek without a paddle. Surprisingly Naomi just nodded after a moment.

"Sure," Naomi agreed easily.

Felix managed to restrain his surprise at her willingness to play ball.

"Just so you know, though?" Naomi said amused, her lips pulling up into a grin. "When I was sitting over at the other table?"

Naomi phrased it like a question, and Felix acknowledged it with a nod.

"I wasn't watching the mirror." Naomi teased.

Felix wanted to die to escape the embarrassment, so he took a sip of his coffee to cover his now red face. This woman was a menace, Felix thought as Naomi started laughing again.

"Alright," Naomi said happily, once she had recovered her composure.

Naomi pressed her hand against her chin in thought, and Felix watched her closely, the red receding from his cheeks slowly.

"I've never personally had to explain this to someone else," Naomi said slowly, taking a sip of her coffee to wet her lips. "So, I'll just tell you some things, and you can ask questions?"

Naomi raised an eyebrow at him questioningly and Felix just nodded in agreement; answers were answers regardless of how they were delivered.

"So, you've awakened, somehow. What was the first strange thing that happened to you?" Naomi asked curiously.

Felix frowned, he was hoping for some *actual* information before she started grilling him.

"A woman ran through the march yesterday, she was being chased by several men in black suits and sunglasses." Felix said quietly, "She grabbed a man in front of me, then a woman and then me." Felix continued, "There was golden light and then they both collapsed, the same thing happened to me."

Felix stopped talking and watched her, unwilling to give up any more information for nothing in return.

Naomi had said he had 'Awakened' what did that mean exactly? Something that had always been in him had woken up? Did the waking up symbolize receiving the mark that he now had? Did that mean that every single person on the planet could get this mark, or could only specific people be awakened?

Naomi had listened attentively to everything he had said, nodding.

"Interesting, her ability was probably something to do with enhancing someone then," Naomi said easily, and when Felix opened his mouth to ask her to elaborate she continued. "Every person that awakens gets a status."

Naomi paused and looked at him.

"A status?" Felix asked, obligingly.

"A status is a golden mark, it's shaped like a leaf." Noami said simply, "So, you get status, and it does a couple of things."

Felix was running the information through his mind trying to read between the lines.

"The first is that it gives you an Archetype," Naomi said idly, staring up at the ceiling in thought. "An Archetype is like a category?"

Naomi sounded unsure, which made him frown.

"There's like twelve of them, I think. Each one gives you a different type of ability based on the category. They are usually pretty unique with didn't rules and effects." Naomi nodded then blinked before adding. "Oh, and each Archetype gives you a certain stat growth per level."

Felix stared at her, wondering if she was just making shit up at this point, It sounded like a role-playing game thing, he thought about what she had said for a moment.

You get awakened by somebody, or you awaken on your own, you are assigned an Archetype, which selects an ability from a pool that fits that specific category, each category gave certain stat point distribution every level, which meant that you could even level up.

"Do you gain stats per level?" Felix asked seriously.

Naomi nodded easily, probably glad her explanation had made some sense, however bizarre it had been.

"Five every level, you can put them into whatever you want," Naomi said plainly.

Felix nodded and asked his next question.

"What are they?" Naomi hesitated for a second, before guessing what he meant in particular, "You mean the Archetypes?"

Felix shook his head in a negative.

"Strength, Dexterity, Intelligence?" Felix fired off one after another, and her face lit up in understanding.

"Durability, Perception, Strength, and Speed." Naomi counted them off on her hand.

Felix wondered over that, what a strange system, only four stats, it was just like a simplified Role Playing Game. So, there wouldn't be any in-human super genius's running around, unless they were born like that. Were there *abilities* that made you smarter? What governed the strength of the abilities if not an intelligence or magic stat? He could figure this out later, it wasn't immediately relevant, so he brushed past it.

"What are the Archetypes?" Felix asked easily.

Naomi sighed.

"There's heaps of them, I can't remember them all. I was a 'Creator'." Naomi offered, she looked distant for a moment, no doubt thinking about her lost ability.

Felix wondered if that was true though, she seemed the kind to accrue as much knowledge as possible and she expected him to believe that she didn't bother finding out the types of abilities of the people around her? She continued before I could call her on it.

"Creators have abilities that let them generate a construct of some kind and control it from a distance. Like a puppeteer with no strings." Naomi said quickly, before looking to see if I was following along.

I was, it seemed fairly straight forward.

"What does the stat growth of a 'Creator' look like?" Felix asked instead, wondering if she would lie again.

"Three perceptions and two speed every level." Naomi straight up told him, without hesitating.

It could still be a lie, Felix thought, but it might be common knowledge amongst these marked people. Felix paused at the thought.

"What are we called? Ninjas, Wizards, Characters?" Felix asked and gave some examples when she didn't immediately understand what he meant.

Her eyes lit up again, it was a tale he would remember.

"Awakened if you've been marked but haven't unlocked yet. Marked, if your mark is complete."

The 'Marked', Felix thought, interesting.

"What are the people called that have the status straight away?" Felix asked straight away, but Naomi held up a hand.

"I'm going to need a new coffee if you're going to keep grilling me like this," Naomi said bemused.

I just nodded and we got up and ordered more coffee, a couple of minutes later we were back at the table, hot coffee in hand.

"The people that have their marks immediately unlocked upon awakening are called 'Instant Unlocks.'" Naomi said plainly, sipping at her drink with a blissful sigh.

"Anything special about them?" Felix asked quietly, doing his best to ignore the lewd noise.

He hoped he wasn't focusing too hard on it; he didn't want to give away that he *was* one.

"They are supposed to have powerful abilities," Naomi said simply, shrugging. "The marks normally take a month to gather enough energy to unlock, instants just have it on by default, I've heard it said that they have a closer connection to the mark."

Naomi paused for a moment and Felix took the opportunity to speak again.

"How were the Collectors unlocking people's marks?" Felix asked thoughtfully.

They had cut off Shane's hand, even though he didn't have a mark before that, either it was possible to unlock while not attached to a person, or they had unlocked it somehow before they removed it.

"You can charge an awakened's mark if you have an unlocked mark," Naomi said bored like it wasn't very interesting. "If you're an instant unlock the mark disappears if somebody tries to remove it as well."

It was interesting that she would know the answer to that, was it common knowledge? Or was that the kind of thing a *Collector* would know.

"How do you use the mark once the month is over?" Felix asked idly, this was the most important part of the conversation, so he had waited until they were buried in the minutia to ask it.

"Once it's unlocked you just touch it and say 'Status'," Naomi said without interest.

Felix didn't scoff, but it was a close thing, he moved and buried his annoyance.

"How do you level up?" Felix asked plainly.

Felix had been watching her closely since the start of the conversation, and she had been slowly getting more uninterested the longer they spoke, he would have to toss her something interesting soon.

"Conflict, you kill something and get a bunch of energy based on how strong they are. The status absorbs it and once it reaches a certain point you level up." Naomi yawned, checking out her fingernails now.

He had one last question left.

"Any way besides killing things?" Felix asked pointedly.

Naomi glanced up before she realized that she had said something strange, moving to sit up straighter and took a longer sip of her coffee.

"You just fight people or do impressive things, if you defeat someone, or win a competition or something it does the same thing, just slower," Naomi said pleasantly.

Felix nodded, her reaction was interesting, she had immediately gone to killing, even though there was a non-lethal way to level up. Felix scooted back a bit away from her, abruptly aware that this woman was more dangerous then she appeared, status or no, thankfully the sense of dread still lingered like an ever-present warning.

Felix got his thoughts in order, he had a ton of information now, he would be able to come to a bunch of conclusions later. He had a deal to uphold now and then he was going to get out of here. Felix cleared his throat and Naomi watched him carefully, curious as to why he had backed away on the chair.

"Yesterday, I went to watch the march." Felix said plainly, "During the march a woman grabbed me, and I was knocked unconscious along with two others."

Naomi nodded easily; I'd already said this part earlier, what I hadn't told her was what had happened next.

"I woke up in a room with around one hundred people," Felix said easily.

It was a little bit of an underestimation, but it made things simpler, Naomi's eyebrows shot up and her lips twitched for a second as she seemingly fought down a smile.

"One hundred!?" Naomi said in surprise, allowing her mouth to fall open.

Felix nodded, her feigned responses just made him warier of her.

"The only door in the room was locked and we were stuck there for hours before the PA system finally turned on," Felix said idly, thinking back to the room. "They asked for the instant unlocks to leave first. Any idea what happened to them?"

Felix snuck in the question and was rewarded with an answer.

"They would have sent them off to the Guild with their memories wiped, standard practice, they can't remove their status," Naomi said easily.

Felix was glad that they hadn't been killed at least, but getting confirmation of the existence of memory wiping was useful information. He had noticed that she had also said, standard practice, which indicated that she might have been involved with them in the past, which just helped him keep his guard up.

What exactly was there version of a 'Guild?' There was a guild in just about every single MMORPG, just a group of characters or players bound together by a name for a group benefit or territory battles. Single-player role-playing games had a guild as a place where people joined or formed a group for a specific goal, like a wizard's guild for people who practiced magic and accrued magical knowledge, or a thief's guild for people with those proclivities. It was just another thing he would have to investigate later.

"We were let out, one person at a time. They said if we tried to go out faster we would be in danger. It took roughly ten minutes between each person" Felix made sure to include a lot of random detail to make it seem as if he was telling her a lot more than she had asked for.

Judging by Naomi's reaction, she knew something about that whether from a perspective of a Collector or from someone who had there turn in the room he still wasn't sure.

"There was something in the room as well, it looked like a person," Felix said slowly.

Naomi tilted her head and was no doubt starting to make the connection.

"It wasn't though, and it ended up killing everyone in the building." Felix finished after a moment.

Naomi was quiet for a long time.

"It didn't kill *you*," Naomi said calmly, it wasn't quite an accusation, but it felt like one to Felix.

"We were the last two in the room and I was determined on going last. It did decide to come after me near the end, but the doors opened, and it left instead; guess it didn't have time to waste on a lowly awakened." Felix said simply, vividly remembering the scene.

"Did you notice anything about it that was peculiar? How did you know it wasn't a person?" Naomi asked she sounded different now, sharper, more calculating.

Felix had to remember that she was an amazing actor because if he forgot he was sure he would end up regretting it, the dread did help.

"It kept giggling, and it had far too many teeth," Felix replied quietly, fighting down a shiver.

"One of the Sin, probably, or a monster of some sort." Naomi said thoughtfully, before pausing, "Or both."

Monsters and Sins.

That seemed like a glaring hole he'd somehow missed during their conversation, what else hadn't she mentioned? Felix couldn't think about it now, so he let it go.

"I left the room after everyone had been killed, all of the bodies had pieces removed, or eaten," Felix said quietly.

"Doesn't narrow it down that much, Monsters and Sin's both eat marks, humans and each other," Naomi said slowly, sitting back in her chair.

That was interesting, they ate marks, eating something indicated a need for sustenance, so it must have provided some sort of energy. Although maybe it just tasted nice, Felix thought.

"Do monsters and Sins both have status?" Felix slipped in another question and she nodded again, and his mind went into overdrive.

What did that mean? They absorbed the power from the status, or it was food or something for them, could humans do that? Was that what the collectors were doing, cutting off people's arms and legs and then eating them? Selling them to the highest bidder? Is that what Naomi was trying to do? Find someone with a mark she could eat?

Felix was suddenly glad he hadn't told her that he was an Instant Unlock, she wouldn't have explained anything if he had revealed it at the start, he would have been useless to her. Naomi noticed his expression and tilted her head again, it had seemed an almost innocent gesture earlier, now it was terrifying.

Felix stared at her for a long while before asking the question he'd been dreading.

"If a human loses their status can they take someone else's?" Felix asked carefully, but the subtext was clear; was she looking for someone to eat?

Naomi stared back at him.

"Yes," Naomi said curiously.

A hidden society filled with cannibal people, 'Monsters', and whatever a 'Sin' was.

Felix forced himself to relax into his chair, there was an easy way to nip this in the bud. He hadn't wanted to mention it, but if the alternative was that Naomi came looking for a snack in a month, he didn't have a choice.

"I lied earlier," Felix said easily while kicking his shoe off under the table.

He reached down and tugged his sock off.

"There were three people who instantly unlocked in the room yesterday, not two," Felix said simply.

Naomi stared down at the golden leaf that sat on the sole of his foot before she sagged back into her chair looking upset, Felix retrieved his shoe and tugged it back on.

"Well shit." Naomi hissed, "That's annoying."

Felix and the now revealed cannibal sat quietly in the café watching each other, Naomi's body language slowly changed, the pleasant demeanor vanishing, and her eyes became sharp and calculating, the only thing real about her had been the boredom. At least he could be certain that she wasn't with the collectors now, if she had wanted a mark to eat, surely they would have provided her with one.

There was something wrong with Naomi though, although he didn't know what it was exactly, the faint sense of dread my be an indication of how strong the person with the mark was for all he knew, or it could be something completely different. Either way, he had felt no anxiousness or panic, and she hadn't shown a hint of what she had been planning on her face or body language. If the sense of dread hadn't been there, he wouldn't have had any idea that she was acting in the first place.

Felix wondered if she even knew that it was there?

Naomi had been planning on talking with him, following him home and in a month when his mark unlocked, eating him. How strange that he couldn't speak with a barista without mumbling or having a panic attack, but he could trade barbs easily with a cannibal without a sign of his anxiety.

Naomi sighed suddenly, looking defeated.

"All of this for nothing huh? It seems like such a waste." Naomi said resignedly.

Felix didn't think it was a waste, but then again *he'd* gotten exactly what he wanted out of the talk, but not *everything* he wanted.

"I have some more questions if you feel like answering." Felix tossed out, to see her reaction if nothing else.

"Nothing in it for me anymore," Naomi huffed, keeping one eye on him as she started to get her things together.

"Give me one moment please, maybe I can make it worth your while," Felix said plainly while holding up a hand and Naomi raised an eyebrow for a moment before she sat back down curiously.

Felix thought as quickly as he could, this woman was a source of information that he couldn't afford to let just walk away.

What did Naomi want?

A status, to get one; she needed to eat one that belonged to someone else, she had mentioned a 'Guild' earlier, which must contain other Status users. This was more evidence towards a larger hidden society, if there *was* a large society, it indicated that there must be a source of trading between the people.

I'd thought briefly that the collectors might have been selling the marks to the highest bidder, which was looking increasingly more likely. If this was the case, why hadn't Naomi simply purchased one from the collectors?

If a lack of funds was the issue, perhaps he could provide the money in exchange for information. He had a large sum saved up, having lived below his means for a long time. He rarely went outside, other than to go to work and so he had spent barely any of his money. He held no attachment to it like he held no attachment to anything else in his miserable life.

He studied Naomi for a moment, she wore brand name clothes and her phone was the newest model, she had a few small pieces of expensive-looking jewelry as well, she was well off clearly; she must have had some money of her own.

Was the status so expensive that she couldn't afford it? Did they pay with something other than money? Or was it something else entirely? Naomi had been fully prepared to murder and eat him not five minutes ago, with barely any physical tells, if she knew where all these other marked ones lived why didn't she just kill and eat one of them? Was she a criminal in the hidden place? Perhaps she couldn't go to wherever they sold the status without being arrested or something.

It had the ring of truth about it, so Felix took a sip of his rapidly cooling coffee before he spoke.

"You can't purchase a Status for some reason. Lack of money seems unlikely," Felix nodded to her phone, "Are you banned or something?"

Naomi looked surprised, because he was wrong or because he was right, he didn't know.

"I'm not allowed in the market," Naomi said carefully, and her eyes were sharp as she studied him.

Market, they *did* have a place to buy and sell things, to trade with one another. It was a society, not just a single organization.

"How about I go to buy something for you then?" Felix offered, watching her.

Naomi snorted.

"You didn't even know there *was* a market five minutes ago." Naomi accused, and Felix let it wash over him without response.

He wasn't going to bother answering that, he currently had control of the conversation again and he wanted it to stay that way, Felix now had something that Naomi wanted and after a moment Naomi spoke again.

"What exactly would you want in exchange?" Naomi asked with narrowed eyes.

Felix thought about it for a moment, what he wanted to be more information about, well, everything. He didn't want to go chasing after some hidden society of cannibals without knowing everything he could first, besides he didn't even know where the market was.

"Information, primarily unless there any other services you could provide me?" Felix said plainly.

Naomi had said that she used to be a 'Creator', and once he found out what *his* ability was, she might be able to train him in its use. There was a one in twelve chance that he might also be a creator, she might have some additional tricks for him.

Naomi let her hair fall over her eyes and looked up at him through her lashes.

"Are you propositioning me?" Naomi said huskily, before tapping a perfectly manicured finger to her lip.

Felix immediately flushed.

"I meant *teaching*," Felix stressed the word, but she just fluttered her eyelashes and leaned towards him again.

"I could *teach* you all sorts of things!" Naomi said coyly.

Felix blew air out of his nose in annoyance.

"Training.' Felix corrected again, then made sure to clarify. "Training to use whatever my ability is."

Naomi was still grinning when she finally replied.

"The abilities are instinctual, and they don't increase in power at all. You simply become better at using them. So, training's not a thing." Naomi rattled off amused.

Felix wondered about that; if the abilities couldn't become more power-ful that would mean there should be a cap on how strong people could get, he wondered how strong or fast he could become with Speed, and Strength at fifty points or even one-hundred.

Naomi let out a long 'hmm' noise, pretending to scratch her chin and Felix rolled his eyes; he already knew she was going to accept the deal, she desperately wanted to get a new status, it was obvious because if he was in her shoes he would desperately want one as well.

"Very well, we have an accord. Information in exchange for a status." Naomi smirked.

The smirk on her face immediately set off alarm bells in his head.

"Can you afford one?" Felix asked wondering if that was the trick, he hadn't agreed to pay for it after all.

Naomi brought her phone back out and demanded his number, and Felix complied hesitantly. Once they exchanged numbers Naomi stood from the table once again smiling pleasantly.

"This has been an interesting day," Naomi said honestly, and Felix could tell that for the first time since he had met her that she was being gen-uine.

Felix simply nodded at her and remained where he was at the table.

"I very much look forward to your call Felix, don't wait too long,"

Naomi warned, before making her way across the room and out of the café.

Felix sat at the table for ten long minutes before he gained the courage to finally leave the building.

When Felix did get back to his apartment, he immediately sat down on his bed and brought his foot into his lap, before staring down at his foot wondering if anything that Naomi had told him had been a lie or a trap of some sort. He wondered if when he activated the mark for the first time like, would something unexpected happen? Would it send out a signal to every marked person in the city that he had unlocked, and they would know exactly where he was? Would it allow people to track him somehow, emit some energy signature that normal people didn't have? Maybe it would simply paralyze him, leaving him easy prey for either Naomi, or his foot might even explode.

Naomi had spun a story that sounded an awful lot like a simplified role-playing game, but in every single role-playing game that Felix had ever played, as soon as the hero began his quest things would immediately start trying to murder him in droves. Technically things had already tried to murder him, the thing in the room, the Collectors and Naomi.

Would Felix be dooming himself if he activated it?

He looked at his foot for a long time before he finally decided to just take the chance, as much as his anxiety held him back when interacting with people, Felix had never been a coward. Felix would deal with the consequences if it was a mistake, just like he always did. Felix pressed his finger to the gold leaf on the sole of his foot.

"Status," Felix said quietly, and his foot erupted in a burst of golden light.

Golden letters and numbers appeared in a grid floating above his foot and they became readable after a small moment. No wave of energy spread from the room, nobody came crashing in his window to eat him and his foot certainly didn't explode.

For the first time in months, Felix smiled.

Status

The Sage

Extend

Level 1

Durability: 5

Perception: 9

Strength: 5

Speed: 5

Points: 5

Four

Felix thought about the mark called 'Status' and what kind of effects it could have on an entire society of people. People with special abilities, and strength or durability that far exceeded a normal human, what could they do? Naomi had said that she had been a 'Creator' somebody who could make a construct of some kind and control it like a puppet.

What was the puppet-thing made of? Was it made of energy or physical matter, a liquid, or a gas? Where did the material to create the 'puppet' come from? Where did it go when it wasn't in use? Where did the energy come from to create it in the first place? In most games, there was a pool of energy, mana, magic, stamina, rage, faith, and any number of others. There was nothing on his Status to indicate such a resource existed at all.

Did it just generate a construct out of nothing?

Felix thought about his archetype, 'The Sage', and what it might mean about him. Were the archetypes chosen based on personality traits? Blood type? Hair color? Or were they chose randomly, or by some unknown metric that differed with every person that awakened. What had determined that he would be a sage, where Naomi would be a creator? If people could cut off a limb and then just eat another's mark to gain their power, did it hold any value at all?

Felix wondered about his ability 'Extend' and what it might do when he used it, he moved the word around in his mind, thoughtfully. It seemed strange to try and apply it as a special ability, Extend, to lengthen something in a direction. Would he become like that stretchy man from the comics? Or that pirate from that anime?

When Felix had activated his status for the first time, he had immediately felt something change in him, like a sense he had always had but never noticed before, almost as natural as breathing. Everything he was in contact with existed as a soft pressure in his mind, the bed beneath him, his clothing, and the floor beneath his feet even the hair on his head registered in whatever this new sense was.

Whatever the effect would be, it worked *through* inanimate materials to a certain extent because he could feel the carpet *through* his shoe. He brandished the sock he still held loosely in his hand in the air in front of him and tugged on the pressure in his mind that coincided with the location of the sock.

A needle-thin circle of material lifted out of the sock and into the air, stabbing into the roof and he immediately stopped pulling on the pressure in alarm, letting go of the sock entirely in his panic. The lance of cloth stayed where it was stuck in the ceiling and Felix watched the sock sway back and forth in shock.

It took a moment for him to realize that *he* had done this.

It was like he had just discovered magic, or realized he was a wizard or something comparable. He reached out and touched the line of material that stretched out of the sock and it felt hard to the touch, he blinked and rubbed his finger along it. The rest of the sock felt just like a regular stretchy sock, while the spike protruding from it was solid as anything he had ever felt.

He wrapped his hand around the spike and tried to break it, but it didn't even depress, he tugged it out of the roof, and it came out with a sprinkling of dust from the ceiling. The entire thing was weightless, well the sock was still the same weight as before, despite there being *much* more material now. He tugged gently on the pressure in his mind and the spike slowly retracted until it disappeared back from where-ever it had come from, and it was now a normal sock once more.

Extend, Felix thought, just what it said on the box.

Felix tested the boundaries of his ability for the next couple of hours and he learned a great many things about it, one of the first things he had done was to try and make two sock spikes at once, then four, then eight, then sixteen and then he abruptly ran out of sock for spikes to emerge from. He could do it with ease, he could also somehow keep track of them all independently without issue moving them all in concert, growing longer and retracting them.

He made a needle-thin thread rise from the floor straight up into the air. He could feel the entire thing like it was a part of his body, proprioception Felix thought it was called. He tugged sideways on the thread and a second thread branched off from the middle of the first. Felix stared at it, before he tugged on the middle of the thread in a hundred different directions at once, making sure they all faced away from him, and the room was abruptly filled with a hundred fine threads at perfect ninety-degree angles.

Felix reached out and gently ran his finger over one, he expected it to be sharp given how thin it was, but it wasn't, Felix frowned. He picked his sock up and dropped it on top of one of the threads intending to pull it tight over it to see if it would cut but instead it landed in two separate pieces on the ground. Felix stared at the now useless sock, and then at his finger before pressing it very gently again another thread, slowly increasing the pressure until he was pushing with his entire body.

That he couldn't be harmed by his power, was the only conclusion he could draw.

Felix tugged another thread out and tried to curve it in a circle and failed for the first time, he was only able to choose the initial direction the object extended, if he wanted to change direction, he would have to create a new branch that started in that direction.

He extended a large rectangle of his floor into the air in front of him the size of a wall post. It rose into the air with great speed until it slammed into one of the horizontal threads with a loud crack and stopped immediately. He couldn't break an object he was extending with another object that he was extending, or the effect of his power had made the tiny thread invulnerable somehow.

Interestingly, Felix thought, he wondered how much force it would take to break something imbued with his power.

Felix retracted everything he had extended, and the room returned to normal except for the little hole in his roof. He then raised a single tile from his kitchen floor into the air like another post and then walked across the room. The tile-post remained in the air, and he could still feel it as well as move it with his power, but he couldn't affect the area around it. He could only affect something in his immediate area, or if it was already under his power before he left the area.

He would extend something later and go for a walk, to check just how far away that aspect of his power worked. He opened the window to his apartment and placed his hand on the wall outside and extended a needle-thin piece of the wall into the air, it shot off and kept on going across the city and into the sky at an angle, with no end in sight. He retracted it as quickly as he could and sat back on his bed.

Felix could think of hundreds of applications of Extend to use against anyone that would come to kill or eat him. He was immune to his power, what if he carried a handful of nails, imbued them with extend, and tossed them at an enemy. It would be like a needle grenade and the damage he would be able to cause would be severe. He could create a forest of unbreakable threads, pillars, or cables in an instant. He could make invulnerable barriers and walls or make handholds in walls. He could leave patches of ground imbued with his power as traps to capture anyone that walked over them and he could control any battlefield that he fought on.

He thought of the needle-thin section of brick that had crossed the city in an instant, he could buy a telescope and a needle and become the greatest sniper to walk the earth with a simple twist of his power. It was both amazing and terrifying at the same time. Felix had only had his power for a single day, he dreaded how creative or powerful someone with a year of practice could be.

There were twelve other archetypes, Naomi had said. Each their category of abilities, what if someone gained the power to transmute matter? The power to create airborne diseases. *His* power seemed to mess with the shape, space, and distance of objects, what if someone had the power to open a hole into space? Were they one awakened person from an extinction event?

Felix didn't know, a day ago it wouldn't have bothered him in the least, but now this whole ordeal had dragged him out of the hole he had been living in for years, he'd felt excited when he first used his power, but now he felt fear. He needed to find out more about the world he had been dragged into, and the sooner the better.

Felix went for a walk to clear his head and test the range of his power, the walk wasn't something he would usually do. He was an indoor creature at heart, generally only leaving his apartment to buy more food, and to go to work. The day he decided to go to the march was a wholly unique experience, and the timing of what had happened afterward had made him wonder whether it was a coincidence or by design.

His direction was towards the largest of the parks in the city, an hour walk from his apartment at least. It took up multiple city blocks and was a splash of green on metal, glass, and asphalt dominated city. He turned the corner and spotted the trees and angled himself towards it. He needed to come up with a plan, Naomi would be expecting him to call soon and Felix would have to venture into a dangerous and unknown world, filled with horrors and cannibals. He would need to seek out a mark and purchase it for her, and he needed information, but to get it he needed to talk to Naomi. This was a daunting task on its own, he felt like he was stepping into a cage with a tiger just being in her presence.

Felix stepped onto the grass in the park and felt a million blades of grass beneath him, all ready to answer the call of his power. Felix was surprised, he hadn't been expecting it, he had assumed that only things that were dead would work. He could move his hair, but not his skin. Could he extend other people's hair if he patted them on the head?

He flinched away from the gruesome thoughts that brought with it.

Instead, he thought about the grass and was privately amused at the thought of growing the grass of the park by an inch, he could imagine the groundskeeper's bewilderment when they failed to cut it. Felix found that he was smiling, and it felt *amazing*, so he closed his eyes for a long while and just basked in the sun. This was the best he had felt in a long time, it was the only positive thing he could even remember if he was being honest.

When he finally opened his eyes, he found a woman standing in front of him with a look of surprise on her face. Felix's heart immediately starting thudding in his chest and all the positive feelings washed away, he felt abruptly guilty when he met her eyes, but for what he didn't know so he looked down at her feet instead. It was the woman that had stood next to Charles at the tree on the day of the march. The woman who had tried to help them up and had gotten zapped instead. Felix realized something and looked her body up and down and tried to figure out why she had every single one of her limbs.

The woman raised her hand and pointed it at him.

"It's *you*," She said excitedly, "from the march!"

Felix flinched as if he had been struck and barely managed to pull himself together enough to give her jerky nod.

"I *knew* it was you." She said victoriously, "What happened at that tree, huh?"

Felix opened his mouth, closed it, and opened it again.

"You fainted." Felix managed to mumble.

The woman shook her head and the hat she was wearing flipped about with the motion.

"Nope." She said immediately, "What was the golden light?"

Felix felt uncomfortable being under the attention of someone so energetic, should he just get it over with and tell her? She had all of her limbs intact, which meant that she was either missing a patch of flesh somewhere or that she hadn't been in the room.

Felix couldn't remember seeing her there at all, and he was sure he would have remembered her as well as he had Charles. If she hadn't been in the room that meant that she hadn't seen anyone with the golden leaf. That left her being awakened in a city filled with people who wanted to eat her. In a month, her mark would unlock and there would be *another* person with powers running around the city. Only she wouldn't know how to activate her mark, she wouldn't know there were cannibals and monsters after her, and she wouldn't know that there was an entire secret society hidden in the city that was cutting things off people.

Felix needed to warn her, he couldn't just let her run off and get killed or eaten, he waged an internal war with his anxiety to just speak up and tell her, but she spoke up before he had managed to get very far.

"What are you thinking about, huh?" She said grinning, "I *saw* you checking me out before, and now there are all these expressions on your face!"

Felix flushed with embarrassment; he was such an idiot.

"I wasn't-" Felix managed before she cut him off again.

"What's your name, anyway?" She asked, before pulling on one of her ears.

Felix stared at the strange gesture and finally managed to reply.

"Felix, and you?" Felix said embarrassed.

"I'm Mia!" Mia said happily before she grabbed him by the arm.

Felix didn't struggle when she started to drag him over to the nearest park bench, unable to bring himself to resist.

Mia sat down on the bench but didn't let go of his arm until he reluctantly joined her, he noted that she was wearing a glove on her left hand, but not her right, the same hand that the woman had grabbed.

"Oh!" Mia noticed his gaze and immediately tugged the glove off.

Mia turned her hand face up and shoved it onto his lap palm upwards without a hint of shame, he was distracted by the faint golden blob that rested in the middle of her palm, barely visible. Felix studied it with interest, it was unnatural and anyone who would look on it would notice the faint glow radiating off of it. Felix realized after a moment that the woman's hand was resting on his crotch and pushed her hand away from him before scooting backward a bit on the bench to regain his personal space.

"She got that blond guy on the arm; did she get you too?" Mia asked curiously.

Felix took a breath and responded.

"Yes." Felix managed one thing at a time. "The blonde man's name was Charles."

Well done Felix, now what?

"Really? Do you know him?" Mia asked happily while fiddling with the dangling thing on her hat.

Felix blinked at that, did he know him? He had met him, and learned his name, did that count as knowing someone?

"I didn't before that woman got us, I woke up in a room with all of the other people that she had touched," Felix mumbled quietly.

Mia's eyes went wide, and her mouth dropped open, she wore her emotions on her face as plain as day, it didn't help his rising anxiety at all, she was too energetic, he didn't know what her responses would be. What if she got angry? Should he just walk away now? Would she *follow* him?

"No way! I just woke up under a bench!" Mia said sadly, seemingly disheartened by the 'missed opportunity.'

Someone had moved her before the Collectors had managed to find her, she was rather short so it wouldn't have been difficult for an average-sized person to move her unconscious body. Felix thought briefly about the room and the horror he had seen afterward.

"You are lucky then, there were over a hundred people that went into that room, and only three came out intact," Felix said it quietly, and with a herculean effort of will forced himself to maintain eye contact with her to make sure that she believed him.

Mia gasped and covered her mouth with her hand.

"What happened?" Mia asked seriously and Felix did his best to explain.

"The people who put us in the room are called the 'Collectors'." Felix murmured, this seemed like the best place for him to start. "The collectors are a group of people who find people who have that yellow mark and remove it."

Mia had scrunched up her face at the word 'remove' and was trying to figure out what he meant by, so he elaborated.

"They cut off the limb the mark is on, or the body part in some cases, there was a man who was touched on the face," Felix swallowed, and paused for a moment in thought.

Where was the most common place to receive a mark? If you got to *choose* where it was placed, did you hide it somewhere out of sight in the hopes nobody found it if you were at their mercy it probably wouldn't matter or would you put it in a place that you could still live your life in relative comfort if they took the limb? Mia was unaware of his morbid thoughts; she had instead leaned forward and was studying him closely.

Felix realized that she was probably trying to locate where he had his mark removed, all four of his limbs were present and he had no visible wounds, she was still uninformed about the state of those who had gotten out intact.

Mia suddenly glanced down at his lap with a sad expression on her face and he flinched

"Did they cut off your thingy?" Mia said weakly.

Felix immediately flushed and scooted even further away from her.

"Of course not!" Felix said embarrassedly, feeling somehow personally attacked by the comment. "I was one of the people who got out *intact*, why would you even think that in the first place?"

Felix was spending a lot of time embarrassed lately.

"Oh! That's good then," Mia said sounding relieved. "Where's *your* mark then?"

Felix reached down and awkwardly tugged off his shoe, took a moment to pull down his sock slightly, and pointed his foot at her, Mia immediately lunged at his foot to get a better look and he snapped his sock back on before quickly pulling his shoe back onto his foot.

"Your one looks like a leaf! Mine just looks like a bruise." Mia said excitedly, before finishing with a pout.

"When someone gets marked it takes a month to unlock, mine is what an unlocked one looks like," Felix mumbled. "Yours will look like mine then."

Mia's stared down at the faint golden blob on her hand with a frown before she turned and stuck her hand in his face, he tried to move back but she followed him along the bench until there was no more bench left.

"Isn't there some way to speed it up? I don't want to wait a month, that's boring! How did you do it, huh? What's your secret?" Mia shot off the barrage of questions with a smile.

Felix was panicking at the proximity and tried to lean away from her hand.

"Hold on a minute!" Felix squeaked, but it came out muffled from behind her hand before Mia pulled back slightly to let him speak. "Supposedly a person who has already unlocked their mark can charge it up."

Mia's eyes lit up and she waved her palm around in his face.

"You can do it then, right? How do we do it?" Mia said excitedly.

Felix didn't know, Naomi hadn't explained that part, but he thought you would *probably* need to touch the mark to an unlocked one.

"I don't know," Felix said instead.

"Maybe you just need to rub it or something?" Mia wondered before she dropped her hand back onto his lap and stared at him expectantly.

Felix swallowed again before he reached down and rubbed the tip of his finger over her palm gently, but nothing happened.

"Well, that didn't work." Mia frowned and scrunched up her face in thought. "Maybe I should touch your mark with mine?"

Felix was honestly surprised she'd come to the same conclusion as he had, she kept saying and doing silly things and he was underestimating her because of it, he vowed to take her more seriously. Felix nodded at her awkwardly and pulled off his shoe again, feeling self-conscious.

Mia snatched his foot up immediately and placed it in her lap and he twitched violently at the sudden movement but managed to restrain himself from pushing her off of him. Mia tugged his sock off and wrapped her cold hand around his foot and Felix felt mortified before the ever-present tingle in his foot immediately started to send pleasant jolts up his leg.

"Oh! That felt nice." Mia said in surprise and pulled her hand back to stare at the perfect golden leaf on her palm.

Felix stared at it as well, surprised it had been so easy, but then again if it had been *difficult* then the Collectors wouldn't have been able to process so many people in a day. Mia turned to look at him with a mischievous look on her freckled face.

Oh no, Felix thought.

"Imagine what this would have been like; if that lady *had* grabbed you on the thingy?" Mia said mischievously.

Felix flushed again and abruptly stood up.

"You can activate it by pressing it and saying status," Felix said quietly. "I have somewhere I need to go, goodbye."

Felix practically fled the park after that, and Mia called something after him but he ignored her. Instead, he angled himself in the direction of the 'Bust a Bean!' from the other day. He funneled all of his embarrassment and annoyance into a ball and used it as fuel to pull out his phone and dial the number that Naomi had given him, she picked up on the second ring.

"Felix, I was wondering if I would have had to come looking for you," Noami said pleasantly.

Felix shivered at the chilling words, he was glad he had decided to call if that was the case, he had some additional motivation now as well, the faster he got Naomi a mark the safer anyone else in this city who had one, like Mia, would be.

"I'm glad you didn't," Felix said quietly and Naomi scoffed.

"That's a terrible thing to say to a girl," Naomi said amused.

Felix thought about what he wanted to do and then decided to rip off the bandaid in a single go.

"I was thinking of going shopping," Felix said plainly, and she read between the lines. "If you're interested, I'll be at the café."

Felix hung up afterward, unable to stomach the conversation without the aura of dread pressing down on him. It would be interesting to see how long it took her to get there, he did not doubt that she *would* come.

Felix tried to imagine what it would be like, to have lived as a superhuman, and then to have it taken away from you, he would have been sprinting to the café if someone had offered to bring it all back. Felix was only a couple of blocks or so away from it, so he didn't have to rush and when he did enter the café, he was only slightly surprised to see that he had beaten Naomi there, it just meant that she had been further away than he was.

Felix approached the counter, which was being taken care of by the same barista as the last time he was there and she smiled at him as he approached, and he mumbled out his order of a white vanilla latte before going to claim the same corner table as before, not even two minutes later Naomi stepped through the door breathing slightly unevenly.

Naomi was dressed in tight jeans, a black shirt with sleeves that reached past her fingertips, and a shoulder bag secured around her torso, her hair was twisted into a spiral on the side of her head, and she had a light layer of perspiration on her skin, the rushed appearance indicated that she had to move fast to get here, and she was sweating so she had either run or walked briskly.

Felix studied her closely, she had arrived within twenty minutes of his call, and the bag she held with her likely had the money he needed to purchase the mark. So, she had come from her house, within one or two miles; depending on how fast she had been moving. It gave Felix an idea of where to avoid if he never wanted to bump into her again it was a shame though, he liked this café.

Naomi ordered something at the counter and talked with the barista for a moment before walking over to his table. The barista was making 'aw' faces at the two of them and Felix had to look away to avoid flushing again. The sense of dread he felt around her had immediately appeared when she stepped into the café, and his mind sharpened with every step she took towards him, reaching a crescendo when she sat down next to him.

"Did you enjoy the walk?" Felix said plainly, fishing for a reaction.

Naomi raised an eyebrow at him, before nodding.

"I was nearby so I thought I may as well." Naomi breathed.

Bullshit, Felix thought, but it didn't matter, he nodded to the bag and Naomi placed it down in between them.

"The payment, it should be enough for any of the mid tiered stuff, fifteen thousand cash," Naomi said easily.

He assumed she was talking about the usefulness of the ability, or how powerful it was, they got more expensive the better the power. Fifteen thousand was what it cost for 'mid-tier' superpowers, it was far cheaper than he expected.

Instead of awakening people and then cutting off their limbs to sell, there were other *far* better ways that the collectors could make money. If they went to any rich or famous person and sold them a superpower, they would pay *millions*. Felix would have bought one if he had enough money, who wouldn't want one?

"Where is the market located?" Felix asked simply.

Naomi noised out an 'Mm' sound before she replied.

"The door to the Saltwall City Underground is in the central business district," Naomi said carefully, studying his reaction, "There is a door there, hidden in plain sight."

A door, hidden right in the central business district, the balls on these people, Felix thought in wonder. How had nobody seen them exit or enter this place? There were cameras all over that area of the city. They had to have something like the Otherside Hotel did then, people had simply walked past it every single day for years and nobody had ever noticed it, there had to have least been *recordings* of these places caught by accident. If no one had noticed them even *then*, the effect must transcend even images or videos of the places.

Felix sat back for a moment in thought, a hidden door that everybody would walk past, and nobody could notice if he was a member of a crazy hidden society and he wanted to make it both convenient for members to enter and maybe even thumb their noses at the non-marked.

Felix thought about the area, the absolute center of the city was a large multiplex series of buildings, they all combined in a large C-shape, only the corners were blocky and not curved. On the inside of the C-shape was a large rectangular paved area with water features, fountains, and benches, people would busk there or set up small popup stalls during the day.

The area stretched to the main road, and right in the middle of the paved area was a single large block of black marble with a summarised version of how the city was founded on one side. The other was a blank, featureless slab of marble.

It was obvious when he thought about it.

"It's on the back of the marble slab in the city center," Felix said quietly.

Naomi's eyebrows shot up in her surprise.

"How did you figure that out?" Naomi asked bewildered. "You didn't even know it *existed* until I told you!"

Felix brushed past the question and asked one of his own more pertinent ones instead.

"You said the 'Underground', so this isn't just a door to the market?" Felix asked for clarification.

Naomi frowned at his evasion but nodded after a moment, she pulled a napkin out of the container on the table and started to sketch something with a pen from her bag.

"The Underground is a city; the market is at the center of it," Naomi explained distractedly.

A city, Felix thought, horrified.

A city full of monsters, killers, and cannibals living right under all these unsuspecting people, how many normal people had they taken over the years? What type of society was this? If they were fine with dismembering people and selling the body parts they might well be aright with any number of other horrible things like human trafficking, slavery, or forced sex work.

Naomi continued after a moment, cutting through the horrific thoughts his mind had brought up.

"The building you're looking for right near the market; it looks like this," Naomi said intently while pushing the napkin across the table towards him.

Felix looked it over, the sketch was pretty good, without even taking into account that it was done on a napkin, a tall, thin building surrounded by much wider squatter ones, it had multiple floors and an elaborate glass frontage, if the shine mark's she had drawn on the windows were any indication. The word 'Collectors' was written in stylish letters above the doors.

It would have been impossible to miss in any case, but another problem had just reared its head.

"You want me to go straight back into the slaughterhouse?" Felix said frowning.

The Collectors were likely already after him because of what had happened at their hotel, surely he could buy a mark from somewhere *else*.

"You thought that the Collectors owned the Otherside Hotel, didn't you?" Naomi said with a smile, clearly amused that he had come to the wrong conclusion.

Felix nodded uncaringly, and she explained.

"They have nothing to do with each other in truth, the Otherside is simply a hotel for the marked. The Collectors are a separate organization entirely, they simply commandeered the hotel for their purposes." Naomi explained easily.

Felix thought about this, it indicated that the Collectors were a much larger organization then he had initially thought, he had thought that they must have been somehow able to run their business while hidden within normal society. Instead, they had a building right in the middle of the Underground City and had enough power to just commandeer a hotel for there purposes. This meant that the Underground endorsed or even encouraged the dismemberment of people, what an awful place it must be.

"You could likely go into the Collectors building anyway, nobody that works there would have been at the hotel, they have no idea who you are," Naomi said easily.

Felix wasn't so sure about that; people were in the hotel the next day, they had to have had cameras of their own, they should at the very least know what he looks like. Felix let it go, either way, he would still have to go there.

"Any preference on ability?" Felix asked plainly.

If It had been *him* sending someone to buy a superpower, he would have been extraordinarily picky, this didn't seem to be the case with Naomi however.

"It doesn't matter, a movement ability would be nice, I suppose," Naomi said idly.

Felix nodded and abruptly stood up throwing the bag over his shoulder.

"Which archetype is that?" Felix asked his final question.

"Explorer," Naomi said intently, watching him closely.

Felix headed for the entrance without another word and Naomi watched him go quietly, if they had switched places, Felix would be worried right about now, wondering if he would ever see the money, the ability, or *him* ever again.

Felix stepped out of the building and walked straight into Mia.

Felix stood dumbfounded for a moment, unable to believe what he was seeing before a sense a horror started to rise within him and he used the lingering sense of dread and his panic to act, reaching out and wrapping his arm around Mia's shoulder, crushing the anxiety that clawed at him and spoke.

"There you are darling! I was just about to come to find you." Felix said cheerfully, as he led her away from the door.

Mia laughed at his sudden daring.

"I had something cool I wanted to show you." Felix continued brightly, and the razor-sharp feeling of Naomi's gaze followed him until they turned the corner out of sight.

Felix immediately dropped his arm from Mia's shoulder and grabbed her hand before taking off in a sprint down the sidewalk. Mia started laughing harder but managed to keep up with him easily, he didn't stop until they were several blocks away and had several tens of buildings between them and Naomi. Felix went to his knees and gasped for breath, while Mia wasn't much better off, she wasn't on her knees however as she had her hands on the back of her head and was pacing back and forth.

Mia spoke up after a moment once she had caught her breath.

"Why exactly did we run again?" Mia managed, between breaths.

Felix gasped for a while longer before he spoke.

"Cannibal, in the café." Felix gasped, feeling like he was dying.

Mia lost some of her cheer at the explanation.

"Oh," Mia said softly, "was it the woman you were sitting within the back?"

Felix pulled himself to his feet, glancing at her briefly before averting his eyes, she never had the angle to see into the store, and he was outside of the store by the time she had appeared, how did she know? Felix had been watching the street, she couldn't have been outside for long enough to have seen.

"How did you find me?" Felix asked instead and immediately felt like slapping himself for being such an idiot.

Whatever her power was, it must have allowed her to track him, and figure out who he had been sitting with.

"I bet you can't guess what my power does, I'll even give you a hint, it's called Acuity." Mia sing-songed teasingly.

Acuity, Felix thought, a keenness of thought, vision, or hearing. S

Mia could either read thoughts, see-through walls, or hear everything in the city, the last one seemed unfitting, the first one seemed terrifying, but she wasn't reacting the way he thought someone would if they could see his thoughts, he pictured her naked briefly to test it, but Mia didn't even blink.

"You can see through things." Felix decided quietly, breath almost entirely caught.

Mia immediately pouted.

"No way! How did you figure that out?" Mia demanded.

Felix ignored the question and stuck his hand into his pocket, with two fingers out.

"How many fingers am I holding up?" Felix mumbled.

Mia's eyes abruptly turned gold and she glanced down at his pocket.

"Two." Mia said, Felix abruptly started changing the fingers, "Three, five, one, four."

Mia stopped and poked out her tongue at him before that same look of mischief appeared on her face.

"I can see your thingy." Mia sing-songed.

Felix immediately turned on his heel and walked away from her in the opposite direction, bright red.

He headed in the direction of the city center this time, only a few blocks away from his destination as the run had eaten most of the distance up. Mia had followed him for some unknown reason and was still laughing at his reaction.

"Where are we going anyway?" Mia asked curiously.

Felix glanced at her, making sure to keep his eyes below eye level to avoid making contact and wondered at the 'we' she had used. They barely knew each other, and she kept on following him around the city like it was some kind of group quest. It was strange, he certainly wouldn't have hunted down someone he had met only once in the park.

"I am going down to the secret underground city below the central business district to buy a status for that woman, so she doesn't eat you or anyone else that is unlucky enough to cross her path," Felix said quietly.

A million-expressions crossed Mia's face in an instant.

"She wants to eat *me*?" Mia said horrified. "I thought you were joking."

Felix cut across the street while the cars were thinnest and onto the opposite side of the street, the paved area of the city center was already in sight but Mia continued to follow him doggedly.

"Yes, if she finds out that you have an unlocked mark," Felix mumbled quietly.

Mia didn't look very happy at this revelation and he couldn't blame her.

"I'll come with you then, I don't *want* to get eaten," Mia said simply.

Felix twitched at the wording but his anxiety murdered the joke in its bed but Mia didn't have the same problem.

"On second thought, maybe it doesn't sound so bad after all." Mia joked with a wink.

Felix felt his face heat up again so he turned his gaze ahead of him and refused to talk to her anymore, he couldn't exactly tell her to go away, the only person he had control over was himself, and that was barely true in most circumstances especially since he could barely look people in the eye.

Felix didn't say anything more as he stepped into the city's center's plaza, the dark marble slab stood proudly right in the middle of the square, twice as tall as a person at least. It was strangely intimidating now that he knew it to be the entrance to a city filled with horrors, maybe having someone with him wouldn't be such a bad idea after all.

Mia could do what she pleased.

Five

Felix placed his hand against the back of the marble slab, it immediately depressed an inch before suddenly sliding to the side without any noise, revealing a dark staircase leading downwards, he could just see an area at the bottom where the stairs flattered out with much more light. Felix stared down the staircase with hesitation for a moment before he stepped down into the stairwell.

Mia followed him barely a second later and he had to press his hand against the wall to keep from tumbling down the stairs after she bumped into him. Felix stopped abruptly when a person appeared at the bottom of the stairs, they were completely cloaked in some kind of black hooded material, there was nowhere to go except back, but the person didn't look like they were attacking so he didn't turn around.

Mia grabbed the back of his shirt and hid behind him as the person started to walk up the stairs and Felix turned sideways to allow the tall person to pass with a simple nod in thanks. Felix managed a nod back before he released the breath he had been holding and continued downward, glad that he hadn't been shanked before he had even gotten down the stairs. When they reached the flat area it abruptly opened up into a massive white stone balcony that overlooked the city below.

The Underground was a massive, vast thing whose roof and walls he couldn't even see, it was just shadows and darkness to all sides. The city itself sat in the middle of the darkness, a sprawling circular island of light within the dark. Felix couldn't see where the lighting was coming from, but the city was perfectly illuminated as if it was receiving the full benefit of the sun. The center of the city was a series of tall buildings made of a pristine white stone, and the further out from the middle the smaller and more ramshackle the buildings became. On the far side of the city was a large square castle-like building that dwarfed everything else.

Directly in front of Felix, on the platform below them was a bridge that angled down from the entrance and crossed the darkness straight into the middle of the distant city. The bridge itself was a marvel of creation, impossibly wide and long enough that the length turned the other end into a small dot in the distance, there was no way it should have been able to hold its own weigh, with no supports, pillars or cables to hold it up. The buildings in the city looked tiny from this end of the bridge, and Felix knew it would take them at *least* half an hour to cross it.

Humans and things that could only be described as monstrous walked up and down the bridge, heading up into Saltwall City, or down into the Underground city below. People sat, ate, played, and roughhoused along the length of the bridge, there was even a small structure built into it, tents, and popup stalls.

Some dangerous-looking people stood at attention every hundred or so meters on the bridge, with polearms and plate mail, some kind of peacekeeping force most likely. There was a massive green thing, that was shaped like a praying mantis but had the face of a man with red hair and a goatee. People didn't run from it, but they certainly didn't delay in getting out of the massive creature's way. It climbed up the stairs that sat just below them on the next level down, and Mia had stuck her entire torso over the edge to stare down at the thing. Felix reached out, hesitated, and then pulled Mia back by the back of her shirt. She stumbled back a step and grinned at him, and the Mantis strode past them without a glance, striding up the stairs to the city.

They watched it disappear and then turned back to the vista in front of them, Mia was the first to speak.

"This is amazing," Mia said quietly, with what sounded like genuine amazement.

Felix couldn't help but agree with her, he'd never seen anything like it which made it all the more jarring that something so beautiful could be filled with murderers and cannibals. The reality was, this didn't match the horror story he had built up in his head at all, but he forced himself to remember that appearances meant nothing.

"We should get moving, don't forget that it isn't exactly safe here," Felix said quietly.

A society of cannibals shouldn't be laughing, playing and singing with each other, a strange dissonance began to bud in him because of it, and a thought crept into his head had he seen what he had thought he had? Did the room happen, were they actually what he thought they were?

Felix crushed the thought, suddenly angry at himself, what was he *doing*?

He had seen what had happened in the Otherside, was he going to catch one glance of some people playing around and trick himself into thinking nothing was wrong? Felix was disgusted at himself. He shook his head and then strode with purpose towards the staircase that leads down to the bridge, his long strides ate up the distance so he didn't forget the danger once more, Mia caught up after a moment and had to skitter along to keep in time with his footfalls.

"Hey, slow down!" Mia called quietly.

Felix glanced at her and cut back a little bit, and she managed to keep the pace.

"Where is the market anyway?" Mia asked, gesturing to the distance city ahead of them.

Felix pointed to the ring of white stone buildings, right in the center of the city.

"It's in there, somewhere, the building says 'Collectors' on it," Felix mumbled quietly.

Felix wondered how long it had been since Naomi had been here, she had said that she wasn't allowed in the *market* but wasn't it more likely that she wasn't allowed in the Underground in general? The bridge practically stopped right in the center of the city anyway, perhaps she couldn't enter any part of it because of that?

It took them almost forty minutes to cross the bridge, entirely because of its length, and as they got closer to the city the buildings that had looked so small in the distance had grown to tower over them, as tall as anything in the city far above them.

Mia was craning her neck to look straight up at the top of the closest building and stumbled back a step in her attempt, her eyes were shining golden, as she used her power to look inside the buildings. Felix wasn't sure it was such a good idea to be using their powers in public, but he was soon disabused of that notion when he noticed that the residents of the city were using their powers without fear in the streets.

A man was doing some kind of fire breathing to a group of onlookers and they were tossing coins into his tin, a small dragon made of fire winged its way out of his mouth, span around him twice and the shot up into the air and exploded in a startling display of sparks, gaining a cheer from the crowd at the spectacle.

A man in a ruffled grey suit was leading an androgynous being passed them, close enough that he could almost reach out and touch them both. The shorter of the two had horns like a ram, curling away from his? Her? Their? Scalp towards the back of its head, was this another monster or a result of an ability?

Besides the horns it looked just like any other person and the creature was *exceedingly* attractive, the monster looked at him briefly and he caught sight of the maroon eyes and a long lock of matching hair fell out of its hood. It smiled at him, and Felix felt his heart thud in his chest; the monster was *far* too attractive. The man in the grey suit, just a regular human, though quite tall tugged on the thin chain that was wrapped around the monster's throat, and it glowed a bright blue color that was unnatural. The monster turned back to follow him with a stumble, and Felix stared after them.

Just like that the wretchedness of the place had reasserted itself, it was something he had thought might have been the case, these people still had slavery at least in some form. Mia hadn't missed the interaction and was staring after the monster, looking about as upset as he was.

Mia opened her mouth to say something, and Felix just nodded.

"I saw, I'm not sure we can do anything about it right now," Felix said quietly.

Mia closed her mouth with a clack of her teeth.

"This place is horrible, I didn't understand why before, everything looks so," Mia trailed off and struggled to find to the word.

Felix understood entirely, it looked so amazing on the surface, a utopia even at first glance, where everyone of every color, size and shape could interact freely, but underneath that pretty layer remained the truth of this place, a place where people were dismembered for their powers, where they invaded the sanctity of a person's mind to wipe away their memories without a second thought, where they chained people up and dragged them through the streets. Felix watched the monster with the ram horns turn a corner and it managed to catch his eye one last time before it disappeared.

Felix swallowed.

The market was a strange place, there were pitched tents, and pop-up stalls across it all manned by any number of different shopkeepers, a simple large area of stone that was perfectly flat, right in the middle of the city. It was much like the plaza far above them while the towering white stone buildings they had seen from the bridge surrounded it, with alleyways and streets in between them all shooting off deeper into the city.

Felix looked at the items in nearby stalls, there were skins, rugs, materials, and bones in one small stall while another held what looked like claws and talons from creatures that Felix didn't want to ever meet, judging by their sheer size.

One tent had a red cross on it, and an old man sat on a stool in front of it, no wares insight. Felix watched as someone tossed a coin into his pot and the man reached out and grabbed the person, there was a burst of pink light and when the man removed the bandages from his arm it looked perfectly fine, apparently healed. There was a tent with a repeating skull pattern on it, and a young woman with dark hair was scratching out a tattoo on another woman's leg. Another tent sold necklaces, amulets, circlets, and more.

Felix wondered about it all, these things all might serve some purpose that he hadn't yet uncovered. These people hunted creatures of some kind, large creatures in some cases, and then sold the parts to each other in the market, this indicated that there was a demand for such items, that people needed claws, and eyes, and bones and skins for some purpose or another. The skins of the creatures, one of which had bright red fur had an unearthly quality to them, and some had been cut and attached to amour plating. Amour denoted warfare or the very least combat, did they wage war on something that existed outside of the underground? Were there other Undergrounds in other cities? Felix had to pull himself back from falling again to wonder at the place.

Mia hadn't managed the same, she was running from stall to stall, asking questions about everything and anything, she even bought a necklace from a creature that had the torso of a beautiful woman and the lower body of a snake. A half-snake half-woman; It sounded like something from a Greek myth, were the monsters here from those same myths? Or where the myths simple tales that had been spread about these people?

Mia put the necklace she had a purchase on immediately and a blue glow surrounded her body before fading, she was grinning when she came back.

"They take card!" Mia laughed like it was the funniest thing in the world.

Felix was privately amused at her wonder.

"What does the necklace do?" Felix mumbled.

"The snake woman, she said that it would stop a single attack of any power," Mia was fiddling with the necklace around her neck. "But it would take a day to recharge afterward."

Felix stared at the necklace for a moment, a single attack of *any* power? Did it work on a rule? Or was it simply strong enough to block most things before needing to be recharged? He considered getting on for himself but decided to return once they had completed their business just in case he needed the extra money.

Felix had spotted the Collectors building as soon as he had gotten most of the way across the bridge. It was tall enough for the sign to be seen over one of the few shorter buildings in the central ring, it was a multi-floored titan that speared straight up into the sky. Just like the napkin that Naomi had drawn on, it was surrounded on both sides by smaller flatter buildings, and above its glass frontage 'Collectors' was written in stylish golden letters, a single street back from the market proper, behind the first row of buildings.

Felix pointed it out to Mia and started to make his way towards it, he idly noted that it was the same direction the monster with the ram horns had been taken in, and he frowned at the thought. Were they taking the monster to have its mark removed? Or was it just coincidence?

When they had almost stepped out of the market a commotion started behind them, they turned around completely and watched as two human men started to fight right at the edge of the market square not too far from them.

One man had somehow created a spinning orb of water above his head and it abruptly shot half a hundred smaller pellets of water out at a great speed that smashed into the opposing man's power, a glowing translucent blue great shield with a demonic fanged face on the front of it, the man with the shield was pushed back across the pavement, digging two shallow trenches where his feet met the stone.

The eyes on the shield suddenly lit up and the demonic face abruptly opened its mouth and started to fire the exact attacks it had been hit with back at the first man. The water-man was unfazed at the reflected attacks and created a single circle of water in front of his body to absorb it while continuing to fire from his orb.

Just as the man with the shield was about to be pushed into a stall, one of the peacekeepers from earlier appeared next to the water user and swept his legs out from under him with the pole of his halberd, spun once into a standing position and then planted his halberd into the ground in front of the still incoming reflected attacks and they were absorbed into the glowing point of his weapon. The shield man vanished his power a second later and held his hands up in surrender when a second peacekeeper, twice as large as the first stepped up and placed his hand on the man's shoulder gently.

They took the two men away from the market, to the cheers and applause of the crowds. Felix burned everything he had seen into his mind to decipher later, those halberds were especially interesting, was that the man's power or an effect of the weapons? Mia was cheering along with the crowd and laughing, a big man with a loud voice slapped her on the back heartily and she stumbled forward still grinning.

Felix found himself smiling at the sight and once the excitement had died down they turned back to continue on their journey around the corner.

"Whoa! Did you see that guy-" Mia said excitedly, but cut herself off once she had spotted the collectors building.

They both fell into a tense silence, the excitement vanishing, and Felix swallowed heavily, wondering if this had been such a great idea, after all, Naomi had said that they wouldn't have any idea who he was, but he hadn't believed it when she had said it, and he certainly didn't believe her now. If he stepped into the building was he going to get jumped by a bunch of people? All of them ready to tear him limb from limb.

He could see through the glass front of the building straight into the lobby, countertops and people were manning each of them. Tens of people wherein the waiting area, some carrying bags, some carrying boxes, and one person was holding onto a glowing blue chain attached to the neck of a familiar face.

The ram monster with the maroon hair was inside, he had been right; they were there to cut off the creature's mark, Felix felt something twist in his stomach at the thought, the man in the ruffled suit was sitting on one of the many chairs with a happy smile on his face.

A person carrying a box stood up and walked over to the counter holding out a ticket, he talked to them for a moment before handing the box over, the attendant retrieved an object from behind the counter and passed it over, and Felix realized a moment later that it was a card reader, the man took out his wallet and put his card into it, a moment later the man was walking out the front doors with a grin on his face.

Felix felt an awful feeling rise in him at the sight, the man had just sold a piece of someone's body, possible a limb to them, Mia's eyes were locked onto the man as he walked away, and she looked pale.

"What was in the box?" Felix asked quietly.

He had a pretty good idea, but it didn't hurt to make sure.

"It was a hand, probably a girl's, it was really small," Mia said weakly.

"I thought so," Felix said quietly, feeling his stomach twist.

Mia turned to face him.

"They are going to sell the monster with the horns, and they're going to cut off its arm, aren't they?" Mia said horrified.

Felix realized at once just how valuable Mia's power would be to the collectors, she could see where a person mark was, if anyone found out about that, they would either try and recruit her, or cut off *her* hand.

"Yes, they are. Mia, don't ever tell anyone about your eyes okay?' Felix said quietly, fighting the awful feeling that clawed at him for daring to tell another person what they should do, but Mia didn't attack him for his presumption.

She looked thoughtful for a moment, thinking about what he'd said.

"Because they would want my power?" Mia correctly deduced after a moment, "So they could find more marks."

Felix just nodded and watched as the number of people in the waiting room slowly but steadily decreased. The ram-monster was staring out the glass windows at them now, curious. Felix wondered how he would have felt, had he been in the thing's shoes, how could it be so calm when they were going to dismember it. Maybe it *wasn't* calm, maybe the chain enforced some type of behavior onto it. Perhaps it was trapped in an unwilling body that followed the commands of its owner without even the ability to act on its own. Felix didn't know If that was what was happening, or if the monster was just resigned to its horrific fate.

Felix took a deep breath and let it slowly out over twenty seconds, whichever it was it didn't matter to him because he wasn't going to let it happen. He stepped off the curb and crossed the street, stepped through the glass doors, and together they entered the Collector's building. Felix looked around the lobby and there was a sign directing him to take a ticket, so he did so and then moved to sit in the waiting room, making sure to sit directly across from the man in the ruffled grey suit.

Felix took a moment to push everything he was feeling into a ball and crushed it.

"Morning," Felix said easily to the man, and the man smiled back at him.

"Good morning to you too." Felix managed to pull a matching smile onto his face despite the humiliation he felt bubbling inside of his chest.

"Selling?" Felix asked cheerfully, and nodded his head to the monster with the ram horns, sitting next to the man.

The monster stared at him curious eyes, probably wondering why Felix had followed it from the market, but the man just nodded happily.

"I was hoping for at least forty thousand." The man said, loud enough to be heard at the counter, before lowering his voice to Felix and leaned forward in his chair.

"But it's only worth about thirty-five, you know? Trying to get some extra." He said, conspiratorially.

Felix nodded with a lopsided smile on his face as if he knew exactly how he felt, forcing himself to ignore the panic that was creeping up his neck.

Felix himself had exactly forty-three thousand dollars in his savings account, everything he had managed to painstakingly save over the last five years, it was just enough to buy the monster. Mia was sitting ramrod straight with her hands clenched in a white-knuckled grip next to him, forcing herself to remain silent and probably wondering why Felix was talking with the man as if they were friends. Felix noticed that Mia still had her gloves on, now both instead of just one, which was probably a good precaution to take, a single glove made it look like she was hiding something.

"What are you in here for? Looking for an upgrade?" He asked with an easy-going smile.

Felix kept the smile on his face, finding it somehow easier now while thinking about how easy it would be to impale the man through his face.

"Something like that, my girlfriend here was dealt a pretty bad hand you know?" Felix said easily, looking the man in the eye.

Felix wondered why the only time he could talk to people was when they were opening hostile, or he *hated* them.

"I was hoping to buy her something *amazing*, you know?" Felix said wryly, and let out a quick laugh.

The man laughed with him and Mia turned to stare at him with a strange expression on her face, which he did his best to ignore.

"I get it," The man said, "Fate deals us all a bad hand sometimes, huh?" He said, and Felix nodded thinking of Shane.

Mia's still hadn't looked away from him.

"Say, you said your pet here has pretty good power," Felix said wonderingly, and Mia flinched at the word pet. "Think it would be any good for my lady here?"

Felix jerked his head towards Mia, who was now perfectly still.

"Absolutely! For the right price, of course, it's a Magician power; It can make the stuff around it move." The man said happily before tugging on the chain expectantly.

The monster was still looking at Felix, but the ground at its feet suddenly started to rise, in a rectangular shape of the stone. Felix stared at it, surprised by the similarities to his power, was his power that common? Naomi had said that powers were unique, were the rules that governed its power vastly different somehow? The raised section suddenly twisted and wrapped around the monster.

It suddenly made sense to him, of course, it wasn't just 'extending' something it was more like it was 'warping' it or 'changing'. It was much more versatile then his own he could tell already, able to move in any direction and change direction while already in motion.

"Is the material it moves indestructibly?" Felix asked curiously and the man looked at the monster.

The horned creature shook its head without taking its eyes off Felix or saying a single thing.

"Very similar to my power, how curious," Felix said easily, leaning forward to meet the man. "Sounds good to me, forty thousand, right?"

Felix offered and the man's eyes lit up.

"Absolutely! Let's step over to the booth and sort it out?" The man stuck out his hand to shake and Felix took it with a smile.

Mia was still staring at him, her expression completely blank, and he didn't even move from her chair. The man walked towards the trading booth, tugging on the chain in his excitement and the creature stumbled. Felix followed at a more sedate pace, not wanting to seem too eager as the man pulled out a square of laminated plastic that had a picture of the ram-being on the front, he scanned it on the machine in front of him and inputted the desired price on his monitor. Felix's monitor woke up suddenly and the screen changed to show the information.

Indentured servitude; indefinite. Race; Monster. Name; Remi. Age; 28. Level; 19. Archetype; Magician. Ability; Alter. Crimes; None.

Felix read it all carefully and pressed accept again, a large '$40,000' was in the middle of the screen, followed by a yes or no prompt, he pressed yes, and it asked for the type of payment, he removed his card and placed it in the machine, it asked for the account and he chose his savings, it asked him to confirm the transaction and he did.

The machine dinged and a newly laminated card was printed out of a slot on his side of the device, the man walked over and clapped him on the shoulder in a friendly manner while holding out the chain for Felix to take.

"Thanks, man! That takes a load off my shoulders, I'll be back on my feet in no time. Thanks for giving me the extra, I appreciate it." The man said genuinely.

Felix just nodded at him.

"Thank you, it's been a pleasure," Felix said smiling.

The man waved again and practically skipped out the door and Felix realized he was still holding the chain, he looked down at Remi, who was only a little over five foot and the monster stared back at him curiously.

Felix opened his mouth, closed it, and then turned on his heel and walked to the other side of the room, where the hanging sign said 'Buying', heading straight up to the counter and Mia popped up at his side.

"What-" Mia started to say, but he cut her off.

"Not here," Felix said blankly, and she stopped at his tone.

"How can I help you today sir?" The woman at the counter asked like it was a fast food place.

Felix felt sick.

"I want to buy an Explorer mark," Felix said simply, keeping his eyes on the countertop unable to force himself into another interaction.

"Of course, sir here is the current selection of ability's available." She slid a tablet across the counter and into his view, it was attached to the counter by a thin chain, the chain in his left hand felt heavy.

A list ordered by price was on the screen, Felix looked to the bottom corner of the tablet and saw that it said page 1 of 17. Felix stared at it numbly for a long moment before he reached out to reorder the list from most expensive down to the cheapest first.

The top mark was only *thirty-four* dollars, he stared at the description, horrified that someone had a hand, or a foot or something worse cut off so that the Collectors could make petty cash.

Felix slowly scrolled down the page until he reached the ten thousand dollars plus pages, he didn't read any of the descriptions for the powers, having had more than enough of this place. He expanded the details for the one in front of him; High-speed-movement ability, line of sight, can only move in straight lines, passes through the spaces between.

He turned it around to face the woman still looked at the counter.

"This one please," Felix said plainly.

Felix removed the bag around his shoulders and placed it gently in front of him.

"Good choice sir, we'll bring your order right out. Paying with cash?" She said pleasantly and he nodded.

The attendant pulled the bag towards her and dumped its contents onto the counter. He watched as she stacked up the groups of notes and counted them quickly, before placing most of them down under the counter and placing the remaining notes and bag back in front of him. Felix placed the leftover amount back into the bag and secured it back over his shoulder before waiting quietly.

Felix could hear Mia shuffling awkwardly beside him and Remi's gaze felt like the sun on his back.

Another employee brought out a black velvet container, it looked like something you would receive at a jewelry store, only the size of a shoebox, the attendant flipped open the lid and a hand lay inside on a cushion, a glowing leaf in between its thumb and first finger. It was a pale chalky white color, and his stomach roiled for a moment.

Felix reached out slowly and closed the lid before picking up the box.

"Thank you, sir, please come back soon!" The woman said pleasantly.

Felix didn't reply as he turned on his heel and walked out of the store, Mia and Remi followed close behind him and when he stepped outside Felix immediately turned right and headed towards the nearest alleyway, checking to make sure he wasn't about to get shanked by anyone hiding in it before he stepped inside it and then immediately dropped the chain.

Felix reached into his wallet and pulled out the laminated card with the monsters' details on it, holding it out for the monster, who stared at it for a long moment before slowly taking it.

"How do I free you? Where do I need to go?" Felix asked quietly, staring at the pattern on the wall.

If there was a system that kept track of a person's status as an indentured servant, that meant that there was a place that made these decisions, which mean that Felix could probably go *there* and have the monster released.

"Oh, thank god," Mia said suddenly, sounding relieved.

Felix flinched, they had only known each other for a couple of hours, so Felix couldn't blame her for thinking it even if someone thinking that about him hurt. Mia caught his flinch and looked away from him before Remi abruptly spoke for the first time.

"You spent forty-thousand-dollars just to free me?" Remi said surprised, its voice was soft and just as androgynous as it looked.

Felix ignored the question.

"Where do I go?" Felix repeated quietly.

Remi held out the chain to him.

"I will take you there," Remi said simply.

The monster didn't move until he had retaken the chain, and Mia was watching with wide eyes.

"Forty-thousand!" Mia breathed under her breath.

Felix frowned, she had been sitting right next to him when they were talking, it shouldn't have been a surprise to her. Remi led them out of the alleyway and back the way they came, for an embarrassing moment, Felix thought Remi was going to take them back to the Collectors, but instead, they continued further up the road, onto another street and two back from the market. Felix made sure to keep the location of the market in mind to orientate himself, so he didn't get lost.

On this new street, there was a squat single-story building in the middle of all the towering monstrosities around it. The other thing that drew his eye was that there were also many, many people on this street, like most of the others, but here the majority of them had chains around their necks, some had anklets or bracelets attached to nearby benches or people.

Felix realized abruptly that he was an idiot, he had freed a *single* servant, in a city full of them, he had accomplished *nothing* at all. To fix this he would need millions of dollars, all his life savings had amounted to in the end, was a single person free, he could have spent that forty-three thousand on whatever the Underground's equivalent of a mercenary was and paid them to free *ten* or *one-hundred* servants by force.

He pushed down the awful feeling that had risen in him at his wastefulness and followed behind Remi, they were led straight to the out of place squat building, and Remi stopped just outside the door and waited for him, Felix stepped into the building and both Remi and Mia followed.

A simple counter spread from one side of the room to the other, an old man with eyebrows that rose off his face and into the air, his hair was white, and most of his face was covered by a thick white beard.

The man looked up when they entered and waved them over when Felix hesitated.

"Welcome! Welcome, what can I do for you?" The old man chirped.

Felix held his hand out to Remi and the monster deposited its card into his hand before he held it out to the man behind the counter.

"I'd like to free this one," Felix said plainly.

The man nodded as if it happened all the time, and for all, he knew it might have.

The man took the card from his hand and stepped into the back room, through the doorway Felix watched him stick the card into a machine which let out a loud 'Ding!' before he grabbed a pair of glowing blue scissors off the back wall, once he had returned he held out a hand.

"Chain please!" He said pleasantly, and Felix held it out to him.

The man sniped a part of the chain just past Felix's hand and the entire thing abruptly disintegrated into blue motes of light.

"Wow!" Mia gasped at the light show, watching as it evaporated.

"Was that all you needed?" The old man said, curiously.

Felix just nodded and turned to leave the store, he stepped out into the street and didn't look at any of the people still chained up around him, feeling disgusting guilty at his stupidity, even more so now that he knew how easy it was to free one. He could have tried to steal the scissors himself, or broken into the shop when nobody was there.

This was a terrible place, a society that purchased, stole, and sold body parts of living people; all completely legal, a society which thought nothing of capturing hundreds of people whose only sin was to have been touched by a lady in a crowd and cutting them into pieces, a society that thrived on enslaving people and trading them away to clear a bit of debt. Felix thought that for the first time in his life, he might have a goal; something worthy he could pursue and feel like he wasn't an inconvenience to everybody around him.

Felix was used to being dragged through life in the wake of others, hiding away, and letting the world act out its thoughtless indifference upon him, but now he could make a choice for himself, strive towards something like all those people in that march had. Felix had felt a lot of different things in the last couple of days, things he certainly wasn't used to or prepared for, but the thing he had felt most keenly was the burning need to torch this place to the ground.

Felix refocused himself again, his primary goals were accomplished, he had Naomi's mark, he hadn't been killed, Mia wouldn't be getting eaten, and he'd done his good deed for the century in freeing the monster.

Now there was only one thing left to do.

Six

Felix started back towards the bridge, entirely ready for this trip to be finished, he needed to just sit in an empty room for a while and think about everything he had learned, before deciding what he was going to do from now on.

Mia was talking quietly with Remi just out of hearing range behind him, they were both still following him. He had a responsibility to at least get Mia back up to the surface, but after that, he was going to go straight home. He didn't know why Remi was following them, but Mia was deep in conversation with the creature so he left them to there own devices.

Felix wondered why Mia had felt the need to come and find him after he had already unlocked her power, all the way across the city, it was unnerving. If it had been the other way around, he wouldn't have been able to bring himself to go find *her* or anyone else for that matter, the idea felt like an intrusion on another but then again she didn't seem to have any problem with looking into buildings or through peoples clothing so it kind of fit the model he had begun to build in his mind.

Felix wondered about what Naomi would do, once he gave her the mark, he didn't know how quickly she would regain whatever power she had, or if she would regain her old stat points at all. It wouldn't be safe to just give it to her upfront, not when she might turn into an unstoppable superhuman as soon as he gave it to her. He would have to come up with some way to ensure she didn't immediately turn on him once she had what she wanted.

A sudden change in the movement of the flow of traffic on the other side of the road caught his eye and he glanced up, two men had split off from everybody else and were headed directly towards him. They were both dressed in a mismatched assortment of leather armor and they held expressions on there face that looked determined, and like they were ready for a fight.

Felix immediately turned to angle himself away from them and towards the nearest alleyway, and Mia and Remi turned to follow him, quickening their steps to match his suddenly faster ones.

"Hey! Where are you going?" Mia called from behind him.

Remi was forced to almost jog because of the difference in their stride lengths but they both managed to keep up with him.

"Two men just split off from the crowd and started coming straight for us," Felix said seriously.

Mia's eyes abruptly went gold and she nodded.

"They do look like they are following us-one of them is pointing at you," Mia said quickly.

They were definitely after him, Felix thought, they had no reason to sudden go after either of the others, but he had been expecting to run into some kind of response from the Collectors every since he had stepped into this strange place.

Remi spoke up,

"They look like bounty hunters," Remi said pleasantly as if there weren't being chased by the people who might want to visit harm upon them.

"I considered something like this might happen, they are only after me, you should both breakaway," Felix said urgently.

Felix was already mapping out a circuitous route in his head to get back to the bridge with the small amount of the city he had already traveled, if he wrapped around a couple of blocks and then used his power to lift himself alongside the bridge, the bounty hunters might not be to follow him without heading back to the bridge entrance first unless they had some type of explorer ability or could fly, but he would have to take the chance.

"I came here *with* you, I'm not going to just ditch you," Mia said bewildered.

"I will remain with you as well," Remi said pleasantly, a moment later.

Felix felt a wave of embarrassment roll over him at the words, it was hard enough for him to force himself to say the words, why did they have to make him talk more?

"That doesn't mean you need to stick with me-you know the way out." Felix said hurriedly, "You can do whatever you want now, neither of you needs to follow me."

He said as they started to make it further into the alleyway.

"I don't-" Mia argued before the bounty hunters took the moment to attack.

A large glowing green fist stretched over Mia's shoulder and slammed into the wall right next to Felix, showering them all with debris from the shattered bricks. Felix didn't turn, instead, he started extending the floor of the alleyway where he had left a patch imbued with his power.

A large square pillar began to rise out of the pavement and quickly reached about half the height of the building, the sides of it abruptly shot out horizontally and sealed them off from the other half of the alley.

"Cool!" Mia said laughing, she clearly didn't understand that they were in a dangerous situation.

Remi added a second wall a couple of meters his one, and it rose slower but as a single large piece as wide as the alleyway itself, no doubt the monsters attempt to stop the bounty hunters from breaking through the first wall.

Felix headed for the exit, and they both followed him but he had only moved a couple of meters before two large hands, glowing bright green appeared above Remi's wall and gripped the top of it. The second set of hands rose over the wall carrying both of the bounty hunters straight over the top. There was a green orb hanging in the air behind one of the men, where all the arms were stretching from.

The second man raised his hand and a single grey ball shot out of his palm and struck the wall next to him, the ball stuck to the wall where is hit before it abruptly shot another ball out of itself at an angle to the opposite wall of the alley, a chain of balls started bouncing out from all of the previous ones like it was self-replicating.

Felix immediately started raising additional walls to block the balls, but within five seconds the alleyway was covered in the things and they were very quickly being overrun, they had been backing up the entire time and barely managed to get out of the alleyway without getting struck.

The bounty hunters shot out of the alleyway after them, there powers no longer in use and Felix had to dodge around a person and several most before he got enough room to cut across the road with Mia and

Remi were only a step behind him. Felix wondered why the two had stopped using their powers, but the answer came to him a second later; it was probably to avoid bringing the peacekeepers down on their heads, they had appeared only moments after those two men had started fighting in the market.

They managed to fight their way through the throng of people and got into another alleyway across the street, Felix immediately started to pour on the speed, feeling his breathing growing louder in his ears, and the footsteps the others close behind. Felix repeated his tactic and started to close off the alley the second they were through it, but this time it shot hundreds of feet into the air, the shadow of the wall covered them; it rose to the roof of the surrounding buildings and even further above it.

Felix thought about what the hunters might do, they could go over it if the arms stretched high enough, they could cut to the right towards the alleyway parallel to them but that would take them back in the direction they had just come from, or they could go to the alleyway on the left which was further away.

Felix turned right, modeling the hunters as a someone who would realize he would be further away if *he* turned left so *they* would likely cut left and then try to intercept them unexpectedly. Felix then brought them into another right turning straight back onto the street they had just left, they re-joined the throngs of people heading back away from the hunters last known location.

They were nowhere in sight and Felix was left safe, but breathing heavily and sweating. Mia seemed barely affected by the short run, other than light perspiration, while Remi was in perfect condition, not even sweating as if they hadn't done anything more taxing then a light stroll.

Felix suddenly felt a spark of energy jump from his foot, up to his head, Mia likely experienced a similar feeling by her reaction.

"Oh!" Mia noised suddenly holding her hand to her chest. "What was that?"

Felix had a pretty good idea; they had both just leveled up.

"You both leveled up; evading stronger people with hostile intent would be the source; we lost the two bounty hunters," Remi said pleasantly while tugging on a lock of long shaggy hair.

Felix nodded at the confirmation, Remi hadn't mentioned leveling up, which likely meant that the two bounty hunters were similar or lower level to the monster. Remi was level nineteen, if he recalled correctly, which put the two hunters in a probable range of level ten to seventeen. If they were both higher than seventeen, Felix assumed it would be enough for Remi to level up at least once.

"Were they somewhere around level fifteen?" Felix asked quietly, keeping his eyes in front of him.

Mia was watching him curiously now.

"Really, how do you know?" Mia asked curiously.

"The creator was likely the one with a higher level, probably around seventeen-to-eighteen, the Magician was much weaker, level twelve at most." Remi said pleasantly, "I'm surprised they are bounty hunters at all with the level's so low, they must be quite new."

The words would have sounded condescending without context, but Remi's tone hadn't changed from the soothing tone, Felix thought he had a pretty good idea of what Remi meant either way; bounty hunters fought people all the time in every form of media that had them as a profession, they would chase down people and either capture them or kill them depending on what the parameters were for the bounty. Then they would take it to be cashed in, with proof of the completed deed, either the person in question or their corpse.

The most relevant piece of information you could extrapolate from this was that they participated in conflict every single day while on the job, and if a single chase had caused Felix and Mia to gain a single level, then the idea that these two were likely on the first week or first month on the job at the most.

"What is the average level for a bounty hunter?" Felix asked quietly.

They were back on the street where all of the servants and slaves were now and heading towards the market from another direction, Felix glanced over at the monster after a moment when she hadn't immediately replied.

"I think level fifty would be a good estimate, for one with a year under their belt," Remi said pleasantly and smiled at him.

Felix snapped his gaze back ahead of him, uncomfortable with the sudden attention, Mia dragged the monster back into a conversation which gave Felix time to unpack that statement.

Level fifty for a single year in a profession that involved heavy combat, and as a result, conflict, the source of experience, which likely meant that the requirements for each additional level got increasingly more difficult, otherwise you would expect a heavy combat profession like a bounty hunter to be in the hundreds.

A bounty hunter that had been working for a *decade* at the rate Remi was suggesting could be over level one hundred easily depending on how often they completed bounties, Felix idly wondered what a level one hundred, with stat growth plus five-hundred free stat points looked like? They must have been monstrously strong.

There had to have been diminishing returns the higher level you got, less experience for each fight, or a larger threshold to reach it didn't make sense with the little amount of information he had otherwise. If you fought someone stronger, every single day a for a year straight Felix imagined you would be much higher level then just level fifty.

Eventually, you would start to eclipse the people as your level rose, and your experience per fight would slow, but every single time a person leveled up in this society it raised the speed at which low leveling people could increase *their* levels, provided they could find and beat someone rated stronger than themselves.

Felix thought that there had to be criminals that went around attacking people for experience, or even something equivalent to a serial killer in this place, if they managed to kill a couple of hundred low to medium level people, they could potentially skyrocket their level in a few days and the stronger they got the easier it would be to kill *more* people. If a level one killed a level one hundred somehow, would they jump up many levels? Was there a cap to how many levels you could get from a single dose of experience regardless of how strong they were?

Felix had been thinking of simple humans, but what about all of the monsters or other creatures that existed in this crazy world? The longer you lived the more conflict you were exposed to, and thus the stronger you could get. How long did a *monster* live for? Felix glanced at Remi and studied the monster for a moment and immediately looked away when Remi caught his gaze again.

Remi looked no older than *twenty* at best, but the card had said it was twenty-eight, did they age slower or was she just particularly youthful due to her attractiveness? If there were monsters that were somehow hundreds of years old, they would be terrified to encounter.

Could *animals* be awakened? What if a tortoise was marked and lived hundreds of years in the wild? Would it become truly monstrous? Monsters or any other long-lived marked being could have a level in the multi hundreds *easily*. Felix did some dirty math if a level seventeen had five free points per level, that gave them eighty-five points to use, and that wasn't even including the stat growth per level. That means they could have around ninety strength if they spent all their points purely into the strength stat, likely more if you did include stat growth.

There must have been a social convention on how to place your stats, how would a society like this naturally lead people to distribute their points after hundreds of years. Would they suggest that people specialize to become super effective in a single thing? Speedsters? Bruisers? Tanks? Investigators?

Maybe some kind of primary and secondary system; fast and strong or strong and durable? Lightning Bruisers, Lighting Tanks? Brutes? Would they advise you to spread your points for variety, to cover every base like a jack of all trades?

Had there been lots of bloodshed in the past, as there had been in normal human society but instead with monsters and humans fighting it out? This society can't have been built without any bloodshed, and Felix doubted that monsters were all as friendly as Remi seemed to be, hell the humans were happy with dismembering people and eating them they weren't much better.

Would society favor durability, to try and survive against older and stronger creatures? To keep alive for just a little bit longer, giving them access to more chances to level up? Felix also found it hard to forget that there were things like the thing from the room running about murdering hundreds of people, what level would *that* thing be?

A hand on his shoulder knocked Felix out of his stupor, and he looked up to meet Mia's eyes before flinching away.

"Hey you were kind of out of it, where are we going again?" Mia said curiously.

Felix felt embarrassed to have been so deep in thought, especially when they were still in danger and he noted that Remi was watching them both with a small smile.

"I was distracted, we should head back toward the bridge-" Felix started quietly.

The fingers of a large green hand curled around Remi's entire torso and dragged the monster straight down into an alleyway in an instant, the sound of shattering stone rang out after a moment, and it could have only been Remi being dashed against a wall. Mia took off down the alleyway after the monster without a second of hesitation, and Felix was only a step behind her.

"Hey! Asshole!" Mia shouted angrily, "Put Remi down!"

It was the angriest Felix had ever heard her and it differently broke the model he had built of her, but he didn't have time to study her, the two bounty hunters had managed to track them down again.

As soon as they got away from them Felix was going to give up on subtlety and drag them straight through the market to the bridge.

"Shut up," The man with the green hands said confidently, "Get on the ground and put your hands on your head."

Remi's body was half sticking out of a wall completely unmoving with two glowing hands wrapped around the monster's body. One of the hands was large enough to keep the entire head and upper chest region of Remi's body pinned to the ground, while the other hand gripped the legs. More hands started to appear from the green orb and waved threateningly in the air behind the hunter's backs.

What a dangerous power, Felix thought, did it come with the infinite multi-tasking that seemed to accompany his power? Just how many hands could the hunter control at once? Felix watched them for a moment wondering if he should just attack while they were standing around posturing. He could pierce their legs instantly with a piece of the ground, but should he? How badly would they get in trouble if he injured the bounty hunters? Were they employed by the city, or just by themselves? Would they bring down an entire larger group upon there heads if they hurt these two?

Felix didn't have time to figure any of it out because Mia suddenly charged down the alley towards them, and Felix watched in complete disbelief as one of the hands flashed out, grew larger, and immediately smashed her flat on the ground. The sound of shattering pavement filled the air and a burst of blue light pulses outwards which could have only been the necklace using up its charge.

Fuck it, Felix thought, they weren't worried about hurting them, he would return the favor.

Felix extended two needle-thin pieces of the pavement at his feet at an angle, the spikes pierced straight through the two hunters shins in an instant without a hint of any resistance and out the other side into the wall behind them.

The other bounty hunter shouted in pain and started shooting his self-replicating balls everywhere but Felix had already started to extend the spike's outward into a massive cage of thick cables that abruptly spread around the two of them and sealed them into a box. The green hands that stretched to Mia and Remi were abruptly cut off as the cage sealed itself around them and disintegrated in the air.

The two hunters started alternating between threats of violence and screaming in pain from the spikes in their legs, while the grey balls the hunter had shot out remained stuck on the walls and didn't vanish, but they also didn't fire again. Either the man needed to have a line of sight for them to replicate, or he was worried about a counterattack if he kept attacking.

Mia managed to stand up and step out of the crater below her completely unharmed.

"Wow! Did you see that? Look at that hole!" Mia was amazed.

Felix thought she should be a little bit more somber considering that if she hadn't bought that necklace, she would have been killed by that attack. Remi had managed to struggle into a sitting position but without a necklace of its own, the monster was badly injured, those green hands were stupidly strong, and Felix could feel the bounty hunter pressing seven of them against the inside of the prison he had built around them, but it didn't budge an inch, completely invulnerable to physical force.

Mia reached out and tried to help the monster to its feet, but one of Remi's legs had been mangled, it was the worst injury Felix had ever seen in his life and judging by the state of Remi's shoulder something was wrong there too.

A sudden thrill raced up his leg again and he staggered back at the sudden feeling, Mia tensed up with a yelp as they both leveled up again and if the shudder that had just rocked Remi's entire body, it had as well.

Felix thought about man with the medical tent in the market who had healed that man's arm.

"We need to get back to the market," Felix said quietly and moved to Remi's undamaged side.

Mia helped him hook his arm under the monster's back and legs to lift the monster into a bridal carry and they made a beeline out of the alleyway towards the market, leaving the bounty hunters trapped. Mia doing her best to clear the way in front of them by yelling and shoving people out of the way, and they managed to get back to the market somehow without being attacked by anybody and approached the small tent with the red cross on the front it. The old man at the tent grinned up at them and held out his pot, unfortunately for Naomi, Felix was going to have to spend some more of her money, as he doubted the man had a car reader in his tent.

"Money's in the bag," Felix said quietly.

Mia reached up and unzipped the bag before tossing a hundred dollars into the pot, the old man's eyebrows shot up to his hairline, which was quite the accomplishment given how much it had receded. The man reached out and touched the three of them one after another, and with a burst of pink light and a tingle that raced through their bodies, they were perfectly healthy again, Felix felt energized even like he had just consumed an energy drink.

Felix watched as the mangled mess of a leg that was hanging off Remi seemingly reverses back to a perfectly normal, if now uncovered leg, Felix couldn't give the incredible feat the attention it truly deserved, because they had more important things to worry about, so he lowered Remi to the ground and stepped away from the monster.

"Thank you," Felix said quietly, before abruptly turning to head for the bridge.

It was time to get out of here before something else went wrong, they had already been attacked twice, and if those two hunters had some way of contacting others while inside the cage they could have more coming after them already, likely much stronger ones.

The three of them strode quickly along the bridge, and he made no move to engage either of them in conversation. There was somehow even more people on the bridge then there had been when they had first arrived, and Felix took a moment to turn towards the city once they had reached the halfway point along the bridge.

Felix released the spikes that had pierced the bounty hunters and let the return back to non-existence, he didn't want to kill either of them, and they would bleed out if he left them in there any longer. If the two of them managed to get to that old man, they would be fine, but if they didn't he certainly wasn't going to go back and check if they were okay.

Felix took a moment to note that the city looked exactly as it did when he had entered the Underground, nothing had changed, although it felt like it *should* have given the things he had seen, learned, and done, the city looked just as beautiful as it had before, but he knew that its appearance was simply a deception. The layer of beauty had been peeled back to reveal the dark, deadly, and disgusting layer hidden beneath.

The strangest part was that despite everything, Felix felt like he wanted to come back here.

Felix observed the city and decided that he *would* return, he would come back and see if he couldn't do something about the terrible parts that had infected this place, he would try to convince whatever governing body that existed in the city, where such horrible atrocities could exist, to change their ways.

They *had* to understand that what they were allowing here was wrong, Felix refused to believe that anyone could be that out of touch with the world above them, he would hear their justifications and then convince them to change, and if he failed to convince them, or they refused; he wouldn't leave them enough of a city to govern.

Felix turned around and didn't look back again and eventually they reached the balcony and Felix climbed the staircase that led back out to Saltwall City, he stepped across the threshold and was surprised to find it was now dark, a contrast to how bright the lighting that had still been in the Underground.

How long had they spent in there? Felix didn't know, but it had to of been three hours at a minimum, likely much more.

Felix watched the people walk past the marble gateway, completely unaware of his presence, the strange effect of the marble slab seemed to reach a couple of feet outwards in a somewhat cone shape in front of it, he abruptly stumbled forward and barely managed to stop himself from tipping out of the effect when Mia pushed her way up and out of the staircase grinning, and a moment later Remi joined them. Felix had no idea what to say to either of them as parting words, the day had been so strange and he wasn't very eloquent at the best of times.

So instead, he just turned and walked away.

The only thing left for him to do was to give the hand to Naomi, and he didn't want to keep a severed hand on his person for much longer so it was better to get over and done with now, so he took a deep breath before pulling out his phone, finding the correct number and calling Naomi, once again, she managed to pick up on the first ring the phone was near her at all times.

"Hello, Felix," Naomi said softly, sounding much the same as the last time he had heard her. "I trust you were successful?"

Felix wondered what would have happened if he had failed, but shook his head to refocus himself.

"Yes, where do you want to meet? Not the Café this time." Felix said quietly,

An idea caught in his mind for how to do the transaction without putting himself in any undue danger.

"How about the park, the closest one to the café," Naomi suggested idly,

Naomi was talking about the large park he had met Mia in earlier, it was in the area he theorized both of them could have lived in and it was likely pretty close to her apartment. That was kind of terrifying, but once she had a status she would not need to go looking for Mia or any-one else.

"Yes, that's fine," Felix said quietly and hung up.

Felix turned right at the corner and started making his way to the park, and realized about half a minute later that Mia and Remi were both still following him for some reason. He didn't stop walking, wanting to make sure he could arrive at the park before Naomi did, in case of a trap but he starting feeling a wave of terrible anxiety surging up his chest.

Were they just going to keep following him forever? Was he going to have to say something to get them to stop? Could he even bring himself to say anything? He didn't know but it wasn't a nice feeling at all so he tried to distract himself from it.

Naomi could have decided upon this location well in advance and already planned something to be waiting when he arrived, he was being paranoid he knew, but this woman had more or less outright confirmed that she had wanted to eat him at one point, so he couldn't put anything past her.

A police car drove past slowly and he kept his gaze straight ahead, making no motion to look at it, the black velvet box in his hand felt heavier. This would be the absolute worst time for him to get flagged down by the police, what would happen if he was caught with a severed hand? They would assume he had killed someone, and he would have no way to prove that he hadn't other than to point the finger at the Underground, which they might not even be able to see because they weren't awakened.

Felix swallowed and took a deep breath.

"Why are you both *still* following me?" Felix asked quietly.

Felix tensed after he said the words, waiting for some kind of vicious reprisal.

"We completed the quest, right? I want a share of the reward." Mia said easily and stuck out her tongue.

Felix was dumbfounded for a second, what did she mean quest? This certainly didn't work like that, they weren't going to get experience for delivering the hand, you got it from fighting and winning, this wasn't *actually* a game.

Remi took the opportunity to speak up before he could bring himself to reply.

"I have nowhere else to go," Remi said pleasantly, despite the heart-wrenching line.

Felix swallowed at the words.

"I can give you some money, and you can find someplace to stay in the Underground?" Felix offered quietly.

"If I stay in the city the bounty hunters will likely come after me again to use me to get to you," Remi said easily.

Felix flinched at the obvious conclusion he had somehow missed because they had both been with him the bounty hunters knew that *he* knew them. If they saw any of the three of them again they would all be in trouble, they would be guilty by association.

What was he supposed to do then? Felix thought.

They could have left before they had gotten wrapped up in all this, but that didn't change the circumstances *now*, and he had some measure of a responsibility to make sure neither of them died because he couldn't bring himself to tell them to go away.

Coward, Felix thought.

Felix had planned on hiding away for a while so that they wouldn't keep coming after him, and now he needed to do something about it because they would be coming after these two as well, so he couldn't just hide.

Would they follow them up here? The Otherside existed in Saltwall City, and the Collectors themselves had no problem with operating up here, were there places for bounty hunters to gather up here, hidden like the Otherside?

"I'll think of something," Felix mumbled quietly. "Don't worry about it right now."

He would fix the mess that he had created, he owed them at least that much.

"If they come after us, I'll kick their asses," Mia said confidently.

Felix just sighed, she had somehow already forgotten that they had already almost killed two of them.

They eventually arrived at the park and a thorough search showed no sign of Naomi, and they used the few minutes he assumed they had left to scout out the area. Mia suggested that he hid the bag of money in a bush at the edge of the park and tell Naomi they had lost it in the fighting.

Felix was worried Naomi would see through the ruse, but he could use it to find a place for Remi to stay so he agreed silently. After they had investigated the area, and Remi had pronounced it completely free of traps, he took a seat on the bench. Remi and Mia both stood in front of him but away from the bench, he had managed to get them to promise not to involve themselves in the discussion but they hadn't wanted to leave the area. Felix had placed the Collector's box on the park bench next to him and extended a tight cage of spikes around it making it completely impossible for anyone to move until he released it.

Naomi arrived minutes later, dressed in the same clothing from earlier in the day, minus the bag that Felix had hidden away, she stopped a couple of meters away from the three of them and studied them intently for a moment, giving a lot more attention to Remi in particular, specifically her hood.

"You certainly didn't say anything about bringing friends." Naomi said languidly, completely at ease, "I do hope this isn't an ambush."

Naomi said it with a smile that showed plenty of teeth, and whereas her body language proclaimed that she was completely relaxed, her eyes were sharp and darting back and forth investigating them and searching the surroundings as if waiting for even more people to step out from behind the trees.

The familiar well of dread had risen with her arrival and his anxiousness evaporated in an instant.

"Don't worry about them, they helped me get the mark for you, it was a lot tougher than anticipated," Felix said casually. "They are *completely* off-limits."

Felix stressed the word and stared directly at her to make sure she understood just how serious he was being, but Naomi just nodded without care.

"They have nothing I want, or need, I'll leave them be." Naomi agreed plainly.

Felix nodded at her, accepting it at face value because it held a ring of truth to it.

"The mark is in this box; I've locked it down with my power," Felix said simply. "I'll release it to you once we are finished here."

The box had 'Collectors' written in white font on the box and it was just visible through a gap in the top before he sealed it shut again.

"Once we are sufficiently out of range, and you'll get the mark. Acceptable?" Felix said easily.

Mia and Remi were both staring at him for some reason, with very strange looks on their faces, had he missed something?

"Those sound-like appropriate precautions to take, I'll play along." Naomi smiled like a predator.

You don't have a choice, Felix thought but didn't say.

"I'd like to talk about some things first before we finish our transaction, I won't take up much of your time, however," Felix said simply.

Naomi nodded and stepped forwards towards him without fear, she sat down next to the box and placed her hand gently on top, he could feel the gentle pressure through his power, it felt almost intimate.

"I expected as much, I *did* promise you information after all, though given your perceptiveness I would imagine the trip to the Underground answered many your questions?" Naomi said intently.

Felix maintained eye-contact with her and simply nodded, the compliment was unexpected.

"Yes." Felix said simply, "There were bounty hunters after me."

Naomi's looked surprised at the news.

"Truly? I would have thought it obvious that you were not responsible for the events at the Otherside. They *do* have cameras after all." Naomi said bemused.

Felix stopped himself from frowning at her, that was his exact reasoning in the first place, and she had known and sent him down anyway, he felt rather annoyed at that.

"Do bounty hunters work topside?" Felix asked evenly.

"Yes, it's exceedingly common for those with bounties on their heads to flee the Underground. There are places all over the city that they could be waiting in." Naomi said easily.

It looks like he wouldn't be able to avoid them by just staying up here then.

"How does one go about setting a bounty up? Or removing one as is more appropriate given my current circumstances." Felix asked plainly.

Naomi stretched her arms up above her head with a yawn and then answered once she had recovered.

"There is an information broker that lives in the Underground, the owner receives the payment for the bounty and pays it out once proof of capture or kill has been established," Naomi answered wryly, "I would suggest not trying to strong-arm the owner, they are very old, and more monstrous than most."

Felix thought back to his earlier thoughts, about the correlation between age and strength, just one more piece of the puzzle.

"To remove a bounty. Well, you'd have to capture the person who set it and have them remove it. Killing them wouldn't work, as the payment would still be around, waiting for someone to cash in." Naomi said easily.

That sounded annoyingly difficult, Felix thought, he didn't even know who had *set* the bounty, other than it was someone that viewed the camera footage at the Otherside Hotel. Perhaps he could ask the information broker? Or pay them rather, for the information. Felix frowned, thinking of a bug walking into a spider's web, would the 'old and more monstrous then some' information broker decide to cash in on his bounty if he just wandered inside its web?

"Does the information broker participate in hunting bounties?" Felix asked plainly.

"No, they abstain from collecting on any bounties, and only fight those who overstep their bounds," Naomi said carefully.

Felix was still studying her closely, so he caught her cheek tightening minutely, perhaps indicating some personal experience with where those bounds might lay.

"Who's your best guess for the person who placed the bounty?" Felix asked curiously.

"I have no idea, it could be any number of people. Pay the broker, if you truly need to know." Naomi said annoyed.

Naomi was slowly growing terser and terser with her replies, becoming impatient while so close to regaining what she had once lost so Felix decided on one more thing that he wanted to know.

"Very well, the last topic," Felix said slowly, and Naomi grinned before leaning forward. "What exactly is a Sin?"

Naomi's grin slid off her face and she sat back with a thoughtful look on her face.

"Interesting question, I remember now that I mentioned it in the café. That the 'thing' that was in the room with you could likely have been one, or perhaps a monster." Naomi said slowly, "Sometimes when a being is awakened something about it goes wrong and the result is a Sin."

Naomi turned her gaze down to the box.

"Whatever they desired most of the strongest personality trait they had before awakening, it becomes their driving force from which all their actions will derive," Naomi said carefully,

A driving force, what did that mean exactly? To be overcome by the need to do something? To be unable to pull yourself from certain patterns of behavior maybe?

"Say a person was particularly greedy and could never have enough money, that particular Sin would become completely driven by the need to find *more* wealth, it would be the force that directed their every action from that point onwards. They would want more of it, and take more of it whenever they could, and desire more of it every moment of their lives, they would steal it, murder and torture to get more of it, their personality would be *completely* subsumed by it and they are *exceedingly* dangerous because of it." Naomi said at length, "The thing you described from the room; it was most likely a Sin based on its deranged behavior and its decision to spare you despite killing every single other person in the building, what it's vice was I couldn't even begin to guess."

Felix stood up slowly, thinking about everything she had just said, he stared down at her for a long moment and found her staring back at him.

It looked like this was where their business ended.

"It was a pleasure doing business with you, Naomi," Felix said simply before walking away from the bench without waiting for a response.

He angled back towards the side of the park he had hidden her bag in, wondering why she hadn't even asked about the money, he picked it up and walked back into the city and in a circuitous route towards his apartment. Mia and Remi appeared by his left side after a couple of moments, but nobody said anything for a long while. When they were about two city blocks away from the park, Felix finally removed his power from the box on the bench. It was finished Naomi had what she wanted, and Felix had more problems than ever.

When they were just a block away from his apartment building, Remi spoke up.

"There was something very wrong with that woman," Remi said pleasantly, despite the chilling words.

"Yeah, it felt like bugs were crawling on my skin just being near her," Mia said uneasily.

Felix had thought he was the only one that had felt it, but he supposed it was silly to think he had been given some special danger sense. Perhaps it was just a result of a massive gap in their respective levels, or a result of her Archetype, or even a left-over part of her previous ability?

Felt shook his head to banish the thought from his head, none of it mattered because they wouldn't be seeing Naomi again.

Seven

They turned onto his street and Felix found himself abruptly in front of his apartment building with Mia and Remi having followed him to the building which made him extremely uncomfortable.

Felix had already accepted that he had a responsibility to at least house Remi for a few nights, and after they had dealt with the bounty hunter situation he could take the monster back to the Underground with the contents of Naomi's bag of money as a kick start to get back on its feet.

Mia, on the other hand, had her own place somewhere else in the city but Felix would never have been able to bring himself to tell her to leave, he couldn't muster the courage to tell her, all he could think was the awful silence that would follow if he did.

Instead, he opened the front door of his building and stepped into the lobby had not said a word in protest, he walked over the tenant's elevator and pressed the button to call it down. It opened immediately when he pressed the button and he stepped inside before turning around out of habit only to immediately realize his mistake.

Mia and Remi stepped in after him and the doors shut behind them, leaving him facing both of them directly and his heart immediately started trying to claw its way out of his chest. Felix refused to meet either of their eyes, instead of looking directly in between the two, and when Mia moved slightly into his field of view, he looked down at the ground instead.

A rushing panic overtook him in an instant as he realized she had moved because she noticed he was avoiding eye contact. He almost wished Naomi were here so that her dread-aura would smother his anxiety, but his almost-wish wasn't granted and so he stood in the elevator feeling trapped.

Nobody said anything for the entire trip and Felix found himself becoming more and more panicked by the second until the elevator mercifully 'dinged', and the doors suddenly opened. Mia and Remi both turned around and stepped outward into the hall. Felix waited for long enough to take a deep breath and then stepped out as well, making a promise to himself to never, *ever* get in an elevator again so long as he lived.

"Nice building!" Mia said enthusiastically, suddenly breaking the minute-long silence.

Remi nodded in agreement at the comment, staring around with interest but Felix didn't say anything to either of them and just walked past them to the door to his apartment and opened it. He stepped over the threshold and abruptly had another panic attack when they followed him in.

What he was supposed to do now?

He hadn't had a guest in his apartment for years, the guy who checked the fire alarms didn't count. Was he supposed to offer them something? Coffee? Tea? Food? They had been running around a crazy city and fighting people all day, were you supposed to offer guests a shower, or use of his bathroom? Felix gripped the kettle on his counter tightly and began to fill it up, by rote.

"Does anyone want coffee?" Felix managed to say quietly.

Two affirmative responses came a moment later and Felix almost breathed a sigh of relief that he had done something correctly, but then Remi spoke up, and he tensed.

"You were acting differently when you were speaking with 'Naomi," Remi said curiously.

The monster said the name with an upward inflection as if to ask if that was her name and Felix struggled to find a response to the question that would need him to reveal personal information about himself to someone he had only met *today*.

Felix was standing so that his back was facing towards them as he was making the coffee, he had hoped that his lack of engagement would force the two of them to talk to each other instead, clearly, it hadn't worked as he had planned.

What was he supposed to say to that? Don't worry, my crippling anxiety just makes it hard to chat, but the dread aura that Naomi has somehow cured it! Yeah, that would make total sense, *idiot*. Felix's thought circled and he found himself standing silent for *far* too long and they had to have *noticed*.

Mia spoke up while he was silently having a meltdown.

"Oh, Felix is just super awkward," Mia said easily and the comment hit him like a knife in the metaphorical back. "He has like *no* social skills whatsoever."

Mia dug the knife deeper and gave it a big twist, while Felix was frozen with two of the mugs in his hand staring at the cupboard in front of him in horror.

"Oh, I see," Remi said amused, whether it was at Mia's bluntness and his bizarre reaction he didn't know.

Felix turned and stepped towards them, placing the mugs down in front of them both at the table before immediately returning to the counter, making sure to keep his eyes on the floor.

"However," Remi said carefully, "Your, awkwardness as Mia put it, vanished during the conversation with Naomi, and my previous master."

The monster took a sip of its coffee and made a small noise of content, and Felix noted that the mug looked large the monster's hands, Remi placed the mug on the table and reached up to pull back its hood, revealing the horns that curled up and backward over its head.

Felix stared at her for a moment, each horn was about thirty centimeters long, and its hair was a dark maroon color settled in a shaggy mess of locks that reached down between the monster's shoulders. Apart from the horns, Remi looked exactly like a human, albeit an extremely attractive one of indeterminate sex.

Their eyes met and Felix immediately returned to staring at the floor, he stayed at the counter but managed to force himself to turn fully to face them at the table, finding himself suddenly self-conscious about the tiny apartment, if it was *larger* he would be further away from them, he was only a couple of meters away at most and it didn't feel like nearly enough.

"I don't know, it's the feeling of dread," Felix mumbled.

Remi just nodded, accepting the answer. And Felix's panic slowly drained over a couple of silent minutes when neither of them made a move to engage him in conversation, and when he felt he was able to talk with freaking out again he took a sip of his coffee and spoke.

"I need to talk to the information broker," Felix said quietly.

He had no idea if the bounty hunters would be able to find him here, but apparently, they *did* come after people outside of the Underground, so he couldn't just hide in his apartment. The two hunters that had attacked them had just been rookies, there had to be others, with abilities that were built for tracking targets down.

Felix *would* get found by someone eventually and then captured, no matter how careful he was, and then he would be at their mercy, and who knows what they would do.

Mia scrunched up her face in thought.

"To find who set the bounty," Remi said pleasantly.

Felix just nodded while staring out the window above their heads, it was almost eight-PM and the day had been a constant blur of excitement with intermittent periods of terror and violence, to be sitting in his kitchen after it all felt surreal, almost like it hadn't happened, and that he had simply dreamt it all.

"Tomorrow," Felix said quietly, into the silence. "I'm going back to the Underground."

"I'm coming too!" Mia said excitedly before she jumped up and pointed at Remi. "Are you with me Remi?!"

Remi glanced at Mia and smiled.

"Yes, I will accompany you both, if you do not mind," Remi said pleasantly.

Felix took a sip of his coffee to cover his mouth, unable to articulate anything well enough to argue with them. Looks like the three of them would all be going back to the Underground tomorrow then. In the meantime, they had made themselves comfortable in his apartment, while Felix just watched quietly from his place on the counter.

Mia started grilling Remi about all sorts of things to do with the Underground, things of more general interest, and the strange powers that the monster had seen. Felix just watched, absorbing the information and doing his best to stay out of the way.

"I once met a man who could create thousands of pink tentacles, not unlike the bounty hunter today," Remi said distractedly, head tilted slightly in memory.

"Wow! That's awesome, like an octopus?" Mia asked excitedly and Remi nodded. "Those are arms though, Octopi don't have tentacles."

Remi nodded seriously at this piece of random trivia as if it was a powerful piece of wisdom.

"I see, the 'arms' had the round parts all over them, it felt very strange," Remi said thoughtfully, taking the correction easily.

Felix was trying to picture thousands of pink tentacles, why would the man have so many out at once? That was a huge amount to have out at one time, he must have had a reason. Felix, almost spoke up to ask about the context, but Mia moved to glance at his computer monitor at the time.

Mia jumped up from where she had taken over his bed, and they both watched as she ran around and picked up all of her belongings and started sticking them back into her pockets, having somehow managed to spread her things all over his apartment in just a couple of hours.

"It's getting late!" Mia grinned before headed back over to the bed before ducking down low to hug Remi. "I'll come around first thing in the morning!"

Remi looked a little surprised at the hug but returned it almost immediately, and then Mia strode up to him at the counter. Felix nodded goodbye, but she kept heading straight toward him and he realized abruptly what she intended too late, and sure enough, he was engulfed in a tight hug.

Felix froze up in embarrassment and made no move to hug her back, but Mia spoke up without letting go, her voice was muffled by his shirt.

"I'm not letting go until you hug me back!" Mia warned.

Felix raised his arms slowly to return the hug, and Mia pulled back after a moment, looked up at him, and laughed at his red face. Mia stepped back and around him before she strode to the door, the two lengths of cloth that hung from her beanie swung with each step, she opened the door, smiled brightly at them and then shut it behind her.

Felix watched the bottom of the door where he could see the shadow of her feet, and Mia remained just outside the door for about thirty seconds, just leaning against the door. Felix wondered if she was using her power, or perhaps only using her phone, either way, her feet abruptly disappeared a moment later, and he was left alone with Remi in his apartment.

Felix wasn't sure if he felt better or worse.

"Mia is very friendly," Remi said pleasantly, from the middle of his bed.

Felix agreed, they had only known each other for a single day, and she was already at a hugging stage, despite his embarrassment Felix found that he didn't dislike it.

"I only met her this morning," Felix said quietly and returned to his place by the countertop.

Remi looked surprised at this news.

"Truly? I thought I had been the odd one out, it feels nice to be included like this, I am very much not used to it." Remi said pleasantly.

Felix nearly flinched at the words, he could relate entirely, having never felt like he had been a part of a group and every day further distancing himself from any chance of finding one.

"I'm not either, but it *is* nice," Felix said quietly.

Remi nodded in understanding, and they settled into a silence that for once didn't make Felix feel awkward, they had all been in here for hours, and it had helped him settle somewhat. Felix didn't feel pressured to speak up, but he found he wanted to this time.

"Will you tell me about yourself? I didn't know monsters even existed until a little while ago." Felix asked hesitantly.

Felix felt silly for asking and wondered if it had come across as offensive in some way, but Remi just smiled at him from the bed.

"There is a variety of monsters, more have been placed in that category then perhaps should have, however." Remi said pleasantly, "We can be every shape and size imaginable; most believe that we originally come into existence through the same unknown power that created the status, nobody knows the validity of that fact, however, but I was born from a union of two others, although I never met either."

Felix ran that over in his mind, whatever had created the marks or the power in them had created the original monsters as well, was it possible that monsters had started as an ability of some sort? The source of the power nobody actually knew or at least hadn't revealed it publicly if they did know.

"I noticed a woman with the lower half of a snake," Felix said carefully, "There are myths in the normal human world that speak of beings like that, is that where the stories come from, monsters?"

"Most likely," Remi said pleasantly, "They aren't gods or demons or titans, but powerful marked ones who have existed from long ago, monster do not age as humans do, we live until we are killed."

Felix swallowed at that, his guesswork had been somewhat correct, if they were immortal then there must be ancient things with obscene abilities and stats that still roamed the earth in hiding.

"There are some who have roamed the earth for thousands of years, with levels that are truly absurd," Remi said pleasantly. "There are the Old Ones, ancient beings that slumber beneath the earth, the sea, and the sky, some of which are gargantuan creatures who haven't moved for millennia."

Felix listened to her quietly, slowly building up a model of Remi in his mind.

Remi was no such being, being young by the standards of most monsters at twenty-eight years old, she had once lived in the far outskirts of the underground, with several others before they had been attacked and enslaved. Remi had been purchased at an auction and then had been taught to read, to write, to sing, to dance, and other things that Felix thought better left unsaid.

Remi had remained in the servitude of the same man for most of its life; A rather affluent man who had long since been killed by a rival, the man had not been nice, Remi had said, but hadn't offered any details as to why. When the man had died Remi had not found itself free, instead, it had been passed along to the man's only surviving apprentice, the same man that Felix had bought her from, he had been a 'better' master apparently, but Felix thought that better must have been relative given that there was slavery involved.

Remi then spoke of how a man and a woman had followed her from the market, they had subsequently bought, freed and then healed Remi, saving her from the removal of her mark, and without asking for a single thing in return. Remi had said it all so smoothly that he hadn't initially realized it had been talking about him and Mia.

"Thank you for saving me, Felix," Remi said brightly.

Felix ducked his head at the gratitude, unable to deal with the attention, anyone with the money on hand would have done the same thing, he knew he wasn't special in that regard, he moved to change the subject then. Felix explained in halting sentences, everything that had happened in the last few days, Remi was a good listener, rarely interrupting throughout, only stopping him to ask a question relevant to the story at hand. They had been talking quite a while before Remi yawned suddenly and Felix blinked and checked the time, seeing the bright numbers showing clearly on his monitor, quarter past eleven.

Felix found that he still wasn't tired, which wasn't surprising after the day he'd had, he already knew he would be awake most of the night, but if they planned on going gallivanting off into the Underground early the next day, they had better try to get some sleep at least.

Felix went to find his spare linen and made a bed on the couch for Remi, he may have spent forty-thousand-dollars to free Remi, but he wasn't giving up his bed for anybody. Felix got some spare clothes out for Remi to wear and took his own into the bathroom with him, he showered and quickly got ready for bed. The monster showered afterward when he offered its use and returned a little while later, wearing the overlarge shirt and shorts that he had given Remi. Felix put the dirtied clothing into the basket to wash in the laundry downstairs in the morning, before turning off the lights and climbing into his bed.

Several hours later, as he had predicted he was still awake while his mind turned endlessly over useless things, it would be one of those nights Felix realized, the ones where he would lay awake and stare at the ceiling for hours upon hours and think of everything he'd done, every little mistake he had ever made, and many more that he hadn't ever been brave enough to make in the first place, he spent hours wondering what people thought of him and tried to figure out if they were right, he tossed and turned but sleep was always just outside of his reach. It was maddening and he wanted to shout at the injustice; but when Remi slipped under the covers of his bed a little while later, Felix found that he couldn't bring himself to say anything at all.

Hours later Felix awoke to the sound of someone knocking on his door, and he managed to drag himself halfway out of bed before realizing that he wasn't wearing any clothes then he froze where he sat, before glancing down to see Remi's face looking up at him from the bed. Felix immediately fled to the bathroom shutting the door behind him, and the knocking at the front door paused for a moment before starting again with even more energy than before.

Felix sat in the shower and tried his best not to panic, it could have only been Mia at the door, and Felix doubted that she had resisted the urge to use her ability on the way over, she would have seen that he hadn't been alone in his bed and the state of dress they were both in, she could probably see him right *now* through the bathroom wall, he wrapped his hands around his knees tightly.

The jolt of adrenaline that had rushed through him was finally starting to fade away and the panic thankfully slowly left with it, as he slowly reached an unsteady calm, as he tried not to think about anything for a while and just relaxed under the hot water that rained down over him, his brain betrayed him within moments, he was *such* an idiot, Felix thought, how had this even happened? After ten minutes had passed and Felix had managed to drag himself out his circular thought process for the third time, he decided he would have to just deal with the consequences.

Felix turned off the shower, stepped out, and grabbed his towel to dry himself off, he looked around for a moment before realizing that he had a new problem. All of his clothes were in the drawers out in the main room of his apartment, while he was in the bathroom wearing only a towel, Felix swallowed and approached the bathroom door, before he took a moment to psyche himself up and then he opened the door just a crack and looked out into his apartment.

Mia was on the other side looking through the crack at him with glowing golden eyes.

Felix yelped and immediately slammed the door in her face leaving him to hear Mia's resulting laughter even through the door, he took a deep breath and then opened the door again, turning sideways to slip past Mia who still hadn't moved. Felix headed straight for his drawers, doing his best to ignore how Remi was sitting calmly on the bed watching them with nothing but a smile. Felix didn't make eye contact with either of them as he quickly picked out his clothes for the day.

"Remi told me everything!" Mia said dramatically, hand against her forehead and pretending to swoon.

Felix felt his heart clench in his chest at the words and froze again.

"How you turned into an insatiable monster the moment I left!" Mia laughed.

Felix slowly pulled the last of his clothes out of the drawer, more embarrassed then he could ever remember.

"I'm not sure that was exactly what I said," Remi said amused.

Mia sighed dramatically and continued.

"How Felix held you down with his big strong hands-" Mia swooned.

Felix practically ran back into the bathroom, slamming the door shut behind him with a sharp clack in his haste, he leaned against the door for a moment, he could already hear laughing again. It hadn't happened like that *at all*, he hadn't initiated *anything* and Remi *didn't* say that, *right*?

Felix took his time in the bathroom, unwilling to hasten his exit back into the other room, but he started to get worried that if he took to long Mia might say something else embarrassing, so he did his best to calm down and then stepped out of the bathroom again, heading straight towards the kitchen while doing his best to ignore them both, Mia was sitting on the bed with Remi now, who still hadn't put on any clothes.

Felix filled the kettle, clicked it on and started grabbing everything he needed to make a simple breakfast of eggs and toast, rather than take the risk of making a mistake he would assume that he was making breakfast for three.

Felix spent a brief moment wondering if people who were marked had specific dietary requirements, did monsters? What about allergies? He didn't want to accidentally kill either of them, he had better ask, which meant he had to speak *again*.

This was hell, Felix thought sullenly.

"Are either of you allergic to anything?" Felix said quietly, refusing to look at either of them.

They stopped their whispered discussion that he was too far away from to make out the words, which did nothing to settle his nerves.

"Nope, I'm not allergic to anything," Mia said easily.

Felix took that as additional evidence that she would be eating.

"I am also not allergic to anything, although I do not like fish," Remi said pleasantly.

Felix felt a shiver run up his spine at the monster's voice before forcing himself to focus on making breakfast, he was immediately tested again when Remi continued after a moment.

"Felix," Remi said pleasantly, "May I use your bathroom to clean-up?"

"Yes." Felix managed, and fought to keep his gaze locked on the counter as Remi walked to the bathroom.

Felix heard the sound of the shower turning on moments later and he glanced up to see that the door was still wide open, before turning back to his work. How could anybody be so comfortable in the presence of others? Felix couldn't even walk through his home naked without being paranoid that someone might see him, even when he was *alone*. Mia stood up from the bed and joined him at the kitchen counter a moment later and he did his best not to react.

"What time are we going anyway?" Mia asked curiously and Felix nearly let out a sigh of relief at the topic.

"After breakfast,'" Felix said quietly before he remembered that Remi had no clean clothes.

Felix glanced at the basket near the door with a frown, they would need to either buy something or wash it and wait for it to dry which would take a while, Mia followed his gaze.

"I brought some clothes over for Remi." Mia smiled, correctly guessing the direction of his thoughts.

Felix just nodded, that was one problem solved.

"Have you eaten yet?" Felix managed.

Felix knew she hadn't but the silence had made him feel pressured to say something, besides he had already placed three plates on the bench.

"Nope, thank you for feeding me, Felix," Mia said happily.

Felix just nodded again and then placed each of the eggs onto a piece of toast one after another. Once it was done, he slid a plate towards her, the sound of the shower stopped barely a moment later, and he turned to start pouring the water from the kettle into the mugs and added a dash of milk to each. Nobody had said anything about not drinking milk so he thought it would be okay.

Felix placed the mugs onto the counter and then Remi walked out of the bathroom clad only in a towel. Felix kept his eyes on his food as Remi joined them at the counter.

"Thank you, Felix," Remi said pleasantly.

Felix just nodded before focusing entirely on his breakfast as the two of them talked while they ate, he stayed silent somewhat out of awkwardness but mostly because he was deep in thought.

The goal for today was to go back to the Underground and get the bounty removed, they needed to find where the information broker was located and then use them to find out who set the bounty. This was going to cost money, and he had exactly three thousand dollars left in his savings account and some leftover money in Naomi's bag.

They would need to hide their faces somehow so that they didn't get jumped the moment they stepped into the city, the two bounty hunters had known what he had looked like well enough that they could pick him out of a crowd, and most of the people down there wore vastly different styles of clothing. Felix had a hooded sweatshirt that he could use to cover his hair and a pair of dark sunglasses that would cover his eyes, he could buy a pack of cough masks from the supermarket to cover his mouth as well.

Felix found himself briefly distracted when Mia abruptly started giggling at something that Remi had said and he watched as Mia put her hands up as if measuring some distance before he forced himself to focus again.

The sunglasses and hood would be the disguise on the way into the market, they would have to find something that would let them blend in better while they were there though and change afterward. If the three of them all went into the Underground wearing the same masks and glasses as a group, they would look probably draw attention. They couldn't forgo the disguise entirely because if even a single bounty hunter of a high level saw them, they would be destroyed almost immediately.

Felix found himself remembering the man in the cloak that had come up the stairs to the Underground, that was the kind of thing that would be ideal. It would cover their normal clothes and the three different colored cloaks would be less suspicious. So, they would disguise themselves temporarily, go to the market to buy three cloaks and then duck into an alleyway somewhere to change into the cloaks.

The next step would be to find some information on the information broker, the irony was thick, Remi might know a good place to start asking about that, but if not they could ask someone who was a regular in the Underground. Someone older would probably have at least heard of them or knew someone who had used their services before. Felix's mind drifted back to the old man that had healed them in the market, they would be going into the market anyway, they could toss him some cash and ask while they were there. If he didn't know, he might be able to point them towards someone that did, either way, it was a start.

Felix nodded to himself the plan was beginning to take shape, once they had the information brokers location, what else did they need? Money, services, or payment, entirely depending on what the information broker asked for.

Felix hadn't been to work in two days so he couldn't count on getting paid the regular amount he would normally get, he glanced down at his phone at the list of missed called and messages, likely from Grant trying to find out where he had gone and why he wasn't showing up for his shifts.

Felix swallowed, he probably wouldn't have a job after all of this, but there may be an answer in the Underground for that too, he had made a promise to himself to try and fix the place so it might be possible for him to get a job down there. Becoming a bounty hunter sounded pretty dangerous, but it would be also a good source of conflict for him to level up, he could make sure he only went after criminals to keep his morality squeaky clean.

Three thousand dollars, would it be enough to find out the identity of whoever had placed the bounty? If it wasn't, they would hit a wall, one that would make everything that much harder they would have to start investigating in a way that didn't use the information broker. That wouldn't be a quick process, it could take days, or weeks even just to find anything of note, and all the asking around would draw attention to them.

Alternatively, he would have to find a less than legal way of making some quick money to pay the information broker, with his power he should be able to cut his way into a bank vault easily enough, or even an armored van. Felix wasn't sure he wanted to take that path, it would make his life in Saltwall City difficult in the future if he was implicated in any way. Felix would try using the rest of his savings as a first attempt, and if it wasn't enough, then Felix would deal with that when he came to it.

What would happen after that Felix thought?

Say he knew the location of who had set the bounty; how did he deal with them? There was no guarantee that they would be willing to sit down and hear him out, it would likely be dangerous just to get an audience with whoever it was, he might even need to capture them and force them to remove the bounty or negotiate with them from a position of power somehow.

Felix wondered how he would do that if it came down to it, it depended almost entirely on how accessible the person would be if they were a low level(literally)thug, he could potentially overpower them in a one on one scenario, his power seemed to be strong and versatile, in a way that allowed him to hit above his weight class.

If it was instead a high-level person, or a person with a high social or political status in the Underground, like a politician, hero, or a famous person he would need to capture them quietly if he could and if they were in a fortified location this would require a proper plan, not just speculation and guesswork like he was currently indulging in. Felix decided that *once* he had the name of the person, he could find somewhere to quietly stay for a little while and figure out a proper plan on how to get to them.

Felix nodded to himself, it wasn't much of a plan, but it was better than nothing.

"I can't believe you left me out," Mia pouted.

Felix blinked and realized that he wasn't alone in his apartment.

"I'm sure you can join us next time," Remi said pleasantly.

"*Really?*" Mia smiled.

Felix didn't have the context needed to figure out what they had been talking about, too lost in his planning, so he ignored the comments, and instead decided to explain what he had come up with.

"I've figured out what I'm going to do," Felix said quietly.

"I think you mean what *we* are going to do," Mia smirked.

It made him distinctly uncomfortable.

"Are you sure you two want to come with me?" Felix asked quietly.

"Yep! There's no way we're staying behind, right?" Mia said cheerfully.

"Mia is correct, I would like to go as well," Remi said pleasantly.

Neither of them had hesitated before they spoke and Felix just accepted it this time. Once they had finished eating, Remi got dressed unashamedly in the middle of his apartment and he did his best not to look.

It less than ten minutes they had packed up everything they needed to the day and left his apartment, the nearest supermarket was between his home and the city center so he brought them there first to purchase a packet of white cough masks and a cheap pair of reflective sunglasses for both of them. Felix privately thought they both looked ridiculous wearing them, but there was no universe in which he spoke up to tell them.

They didn't linger there for long, instead of making their way back towards the central business district. Tere amount of people walking the streets had again diminished greatly, the crowds of people that had been drawn by the march were finally started to trickle out of the city, although there was still a great deal more than was usual.

Felix kept his eyes low to avoid making eye contact with any strangers, but every time somebody passed by him he felt himself become hyperaware of there presence until they had vanished from his sight, it was an exhausting walk to the plaza.

When they did finally arrive at the marble founding stone, Mia was the one to open the entrance, and Felix made sure to leave ample room between him and the others on the staircase, unwilling to make any unwanted contact.

As they made there was down the staircase to the city full of cannibals Felix could only hope that the information broker took card.

Eight

Felix stepped out of the staircase and onto the balcony that overlooked the Underground, it didn't seem to have changed in the single day that they had been gone although it would have been pretty alarming if it had.

"It's so pretty from here," Mia said quietly.

"I've never thought of the Saltwall Underground as being beautiful, I suppose I have some biases in that regard, and I must admit it *does* look nice from here," Remi said pleasantly.

Felix completely agreed with them both, from up here it did look otherworldly and beautiful beyond anything he had seen up above, but he knew that it was only a façade now, one that didn't hold up upon closer inspection.

"Have you ever been to one of the other Undergrounds?" Felix asked quietly.

"I'm afraid not, yesterday was the first time I had left this place at all," Remi said pleasantly.

"Wow, you didn't tell me that!" Mia said surprised, "What did you think of Saltwall City?"

"It's strange to see so many vehicles moving around the roads, as you have seen there aren't any down here," Remi said bemused.

Mia scrunched up her face at the non-personal answer.

"We shouldn't linger for too long, it's still dangerous," Felix said quietly.

Felix started across the bridge and the other two followed a moment later, with Mia badgering Remi for a more in-depth answer. Felix made sure to keep an eye on everyone around him, to ensure they didn't get ambushed because of a lack of vigilance.

They made it most of the way across before Mia dragged him back into the conversation.

"Hey Felix, what did you put your points into?" Mia asked curiously.

Felix glanced at her and found that she was looking directly at him, and immediately averted his eyes, as he thought about the question, he hadn't spent any of his points at all, he'd been holding onto them until he could come to a decision for his future build, something which he hadn't had a chance to sit down and work out.

Felix had spent some time studying his status, however, and had figured out what his stat growth was by for each level based one what he had started with and what he had now. The Archetype, 'Sage' apparently had a stat growth of four perceptions and one speed per level, which was both disappointing and interesting at the same time.

While he *would* get slightly faster every time he leveled, which is something he was happy about as he had always been fascinated by speed based builds, he would *never* have the kind of strength and speed that someone would be capable of with an Archetype that focused more heavily on those stats.

He could feel the difference in his perception though already, he could see further and, in more detail, sounds were clearly and crisper, he could feel a slight vibration with every footstep he took and a corresponding one every single person made within a small radius of him, while he had no proof yet, he had a guess that his reflexes and the tracking of fast objects were increasing as well.

Felix had checked his Status when he had first gotten into the shower this morning, he thought back to when he had activated it, he was level *four* now, and his perception score had rocketed up to twenty-one points, he had eight-speed, and the five points in both durability and strength remained unchanged, along with his twenty unspent stat points in total.

"I haven't spent them yet," Felix said hesitantly, after a fairly long pause.

"Why not? I put all of my points in durability after that green guy put me into the ground." Mia said easily.

Felix nodded at that, it made sense to do in response to almost being killed she had realized it, after all, he needed to start modeling her better.

"I'm not sure how I want to distribute my stat points yet," Felix said simply and left it at that.

It wasn't quite the truth; he was almost certain he would be ignoring both durability and strength almost entirely, his perception was always naturally going to be high because of his disproportionate growth, but if he combined it with dumping all of his points into speed, he should be able to avoid most threats and become somewhat powerful.

He should be able to leverage his power most effectively that way, being able to see and react to things would allow him he could use his power to impede people and strike at them while being hopefully fast enough to block or evade everything else. If this were a game, he would have fit into the role of an assassin or thief class.

"What level are you, Remi? Didn't you level up in the fight yesterday?" Mia asked curiously.

"Yes, I did gain a level and I am currently level nineteen," Remi said happily.

Felix frowned in thought, level nineteen seemed low for someone who had been apart of the Underground for twenty-eight years if he had twenty years to level up, he would have been in the hundreds easily.

Felix also knew that his outsider perspective was skewered though, he was coming at it like a game rather than living in actually dangerous conditions where death was painful and permanent. Most people or monsters in this case would do their best to avoid conflict and as a result, probably wouldn't seek out the fights or challenges they needed to increase quickly in level.

Remi had also been kept as a servant, and probably wasn't exposed to a constant stream of danger, like some who lived in more physically dangerous areas, prone to violence or theft, which begged the question of how Remi had gotten *those* levels in the first place.

Felix thought about what could constitute conflict for a child in the outskirts of a city if Remi had fought off a mugging attempt once a year for every year it had been alive that would put Remi at a level a little bit higher then now. Felix frowned, perhaps most of the levels Remi had gotten were before being enslaved, and then the following years had been in captivity but *not* in physical danger that was severe enough to grant conflict experience. It might have been a great deal more dangerous out in the outer city then it was in the market or surrounding areas.

"I put my stats from this level in strength, to even them out, they are all currently sitting around fifty points or above," Remi said happily, and seemingly without a hint of hesitation.

Revealing that kind of information in public must be more common than he had been assuming because he couldn't imagine just outright telling being where his strengths and weaknesses lay, or even just the distribution of his stats. On second thought both Remi and Mia had done it, and only one of them had been raised in this environment, so he was likely wrong.

Perhaps it was just him being stupid again.

Either way, that gave her somewhere around two hundred points; eighteen levels were ninety unspent points, and if like his own, Remi gained five points in stat growth, that added up quite nicely. Was even distribution the common way to do it here after all?

Felix needed more reference points.

"Wow! You're strong! Maybe I was wrong earlier, and it was *Remi* who held *Felix* down-" Mia said mischievously.

Felix immediately sped up and retreated into his thoughts again, unable to deal with her teasing without losing his composure. They were approaching the end of the bridge now, and thus the market was in sight, they had been drawing the occasional strange look, probably because they were all wearing the same cheap sunglasses as Felix hadn't been able to find his original pair.

Felix angled them straight towards where the stall filled with animal skins, and he found it quickly despite it not being in quite the same spot as it had been yesterday. There was a clothing rack at the back of the stall with simple colored cloaks hanging from it, all with matching hoods and it roughly fit what he had envisioned so he stepped up to the stall and the woman behind the counter noticed him quickly.

"Welcome! What can I do for you lot?" She said grinning.

The stall owner was an elderly woman with short hair that had long since turned grey, but she moved with startling speed for one so old and held an air of enthusiasm about her, Felix pointed to the rack behind her.

"I would like to purchase three of those cloaks, different colors, the muted ones please," Felix said quietly.

The woman's grin widened; three cloaks must have been a pretty good start to her day, which made him dread whatever the total price was going to end up being. The old lady brought them over and Felix was happy enough with her choices. A mottled grey, a washed-out green, and a faded red cloak were placed on the counter.

"Three-hundred-sixty, for the lot." The old lady chirped.

Felix swallowed and pulled out his wallet and counted out enough to cover it from the last of Naomi's money, overpaying slightly when he was unable to find the correct notes.

"Is there anything I should know about the cloaks?" Felix said quietly.

The old woman nodded happily and pushed his clothing closer to them.

"They have been enhanced by a power that grants at least C-rank physical resistance, although sometimes the power is slightly stronger." The old lady rattled off.

Felix nodded as if he understood what that equated to in relative terms and then stepped back from the counter. He stepped around the others and headed for the nearest alleyway, making sure to take in everybody's appearance in the vicinity just in case.

Felix wondered over what he had just learned, there where people with powers that could change certain properties on common objects and then they could sell them to others, that was one way to make money, enhancing the gear of others. Felix thought he might be able to do something similar with his power, if only for himself because he was immune to it, if he made hundreds of tiny interlocking extended sections or even just imbued plates of ceramic underneath body armor, he might be capable of creating an entire invulnerable suit of armor with his power and if he could imbue the entire thing it might even become weightless. If he wore a full-body skin-tight suit and extended the entire thing a single centimeter outward, minus spaces for the joints he would be almost completely invulnerable.

Felix wasn't sure exactly how the effect of his power worked though if someone with a ridiculously high strength stat punched him, and he smashed into a building, would the force carry through the armor into him? Or would it be stopped? He wasn't sure he was comfortable with finding out while under fire, it was something to try out in private first. Felix reached the alleyway and turned down it before passing two of the cloaks to the others, by chance he had ended up with the mottled grey one.

"Thanks! Remi can I have the red one, though?" Mia asked brightly.

"Of course," Remi said pleasantly and switched the cloaks with an issue.

"Thank you, Felix," Remi said softly, making sure to make eye contact with him.

Felix vividly remembered Remi saying something very similar earlier that morning and his cheeks went red at the intentional reminder and he turned away from them both embarrassed and heard Remi make an amused noise from behind him.

Felix focused on the cloak in his hand to blot out the world, and found that it covered him completely, and with the hood pulled down it cast a small shadow over his face helping to muddy his features, he pulled out the package of cough masks he had bought earlier and handed one to each of the others without a word, and just like that they were completely anonymous.

Hiding away under so many layers almost made him feel better, but he wasn't going to assume that they were perfectly safe now, all of it would be worth absolutely *nothing* if the hunters could see through things or had someone that tracked via scent, or some other esoteric power, there was no doubt that hundreds of strange powers existed that could be used to find them, and there was no way that Felix could overall bases, it was impossible.

They would just have to deal with it, believing the enemy unbeatable, untouchable, or in this case, untrickable never helped anybody, you had to at least *believe* you could accomplish the task.

Once they were all covered, they returned to the market and headed straight for the old man that had healed them yesterday and the man looked up at their arrival with a smile and held his pot out, not a sign of hesitation despite our clothing, he must see plenty of strangely dressed people every day, this was likely nothing new to the man.

Felix pulled out the two hundred dollar bills of the money he had kept from Naomi's bag, not feeling guilty in the slightest, it was being used for a good cause, at least he thought so, Felix held it over the pot and the man grinned up at him.

"Directions to the information broker," Felix said clearly and dropped the wrapped notes into the pot.

The old man raised an eyebrow in bewilderment before he scratched his chin, and made a show of nodding seriously a few times and letting out a few deep 'Hm's' before he finally answered.

"Three blocks directly behind you, on the far side of the street, there exist *many* wooden buildings, the one you are looking for is hidden in the shadow of a twisted looking oak, that is where you will find what you are looking for." The old man said seriously.

Felix felt a surged of relief that he had found somebody that knew about it on his first try, maybe he was doomed to fail everything he tried after all? He also noted that the old man had *perfect* pronunciation, every word was perfectly constructed, but there was something off about the way he spoke. It couldn't have been his first language, Felix guessed and left it at that.

Felix nodded at the man in thanks and turned to leave, and distantly noted that the old man watched them go with a smile, but he hadn't warned them of any danger, so perhaps he was just happy with the payment. They managed to go the entire way without an incident, and Felix couldn't tell if it was all about to come crashing down, or if they were actually in the clear. Felix stopped next to a twisted looking oak tree that had speared out of the pavement and into the air, and directly behind it at the wooden building that sat in plain sight.

Felix stared at it for a long time, not saying anything, until Mia finally spoke up.

"Um, Felix? Why did you give that old man all that money if it wasn't even hidden?" Mia managed before she burst into giggled, and Remi followed her a moment later.

Felix felt his cheeks heat up in embarrassment and read the sign that was hanging up at the front of the store once again, but it remained the same. 'Information Brokerage' was written in plain black lettering and he swallowed again.

Felix could have asked anyone in the market for directions and they might have known, the place was right out in the open, without even an attempt to hide it, as he had stupidly assumed. The old man had totally scammed him, regardless of the fact that it was Felix had approached the old man, and not the other way around.

"I spent most of my time inside, so I didn't know this was here." Remi giggled, once she had recovered. "I haven't been to this part of the city before either."

Felix just nodded at the explanation, it was nobodies fault but his own, she hadn't needed to defend her actions he had blamed Remi at all. The only thing strange about this place was the lack of people on the street, people seemed to actively avoid this road for some reason because he could see people moving about everywhere else.

Felix turned and stepped into the buildings open door, the front of the store was small, with just a couple of waiting chairs and a counter that went from wall to wall, but behind the counter, the wall had been completely removed and the room abruptly expanded into a massive cavern that was much larger than could have possibly fit inside the building.

It stretched for miles and then was abruptly swallowed into darkness, it was strangely intimidating and Felix stared into the room beyond trying to understand what the purpose of it could have been when he noticed something move in the distance, a tiny hand, with thin and pale fingers appeared out of the dark, right in the middle of the darkness, with its palm facing upwards.

Felix watched in horror as the arm started moving closer to their position, and grew quickly in size with every passing second until it was larger than the entire front of the building, and it *kept getting larger*. It took almost a full minute before it finally reached the room, and its sheer size had left them all frozen in fear, Mia let out a terrifying noise and stumbled behind him while Remi moved closer to them both.

One abnormally long finger, comparable in width to the bridge pressed ever-so-gently against where the store abruptly dropped off into the darkness and the figure sitting in the palm stood and walked forward across one of its fingers and Felix noticed somewhere in the back of his mind, that behind the monstrous size limb in the far distance he could just see the crook of an elbow clearing the edge of the darkness, just how big was this thing?

It had to have been comparable in size to the entire city above them, a primal feeling of terror rose in him. The woman had a large volume of straight black hair that reached down to her ankles, and her face was as white as porcelain, a bright smile erupted on her face as she stepped up to the counter.

"Customers! How lovely," The woman said with a closed mouth smile. "I am Lidia, the owner of this establishment."

Felix pulled himself together and used the feeling of terror to sharpen his mind.

"Lidia, my name is Felix," Felix said evenly.

Lidia clapped once in happiness and he fought not to twitch at the sudden noise.

"Felix," Lidia said thoughtfully, "Someone who is lucky or happy if I remember correctly, a lovely name, indeed."

Felix had seen what his name had meant once on the internet, and irony of someone like him being either happy or lucky was thick.

"Lidia, somebody has placed a bounty on me, and I would like to know the identity of this person so that I can get it removed," Felix said politely.

Felix couldn't help but remember that Naomi had said that they would not collect his bounty themselves, but the sheer size of the thing behind Lidia had chased any confidence Felix had in the idea of defending himself if they decided to.

Lidia placed a hand on her chin and nodded serenely.

"I see, I see, information like this does *not* come cheaply of course, as I am sure *you* realize," Lidia said pleasantly.

Felix just nodded, wondering suddenly why he didn't feel any sense of anxiousness when speaking to her. It wasn't the terror either, that was completely natural as far as he could tell, the giant thing hiding in the dark was a completely normal thing to fear as far as he was concerned.

When he was with Naomi her sense of dread pressed down on him almost reaching the physical plane, and it had the strange effect of helping him overcome his anxiety, but this was entirely different. There was nothing like it present right now, it was almost like calling someone on the phone.

Felix briefly glanced over his shoulder at Mia and tried to meet her eyes before snapping his gaze forward again, his anxiety was still present, it was just that Lidia seemed to not trigger the same responses that everyone else did.

What on earth was going on here?

Felix barely managed to stop himself from frowning, there was something wrong with this woman, what was it? Felix ran the conversation over in his mind quickly, her words were pronounced perfectly, her movements were all perfectly graceful and unhurried, her expressions were too, but nothing reached her eyes, was she using her power on him? Or using power on herself to hide her presence or something abstract?

Oh, the realization hit Felix suddenly, it wasn't that she was *using* her power on him, it was that she *was* the power. Felix lifted his eyes above the puppets head and stared into the darkness of the cavern behind it.

"Lidia," Felix said clearly to the thing in the darkness. "How much would this information cost me?"

The puppet pretending to be a person tilted its head at him before replying with a smile that this time showed teeth and her teeth were needle-thin and far too numerous in her mouth, Felix clamped down on the shiver that traveled down his spine.

"I would say that this *specific* piece of information would cost *you* exactly three-thousand dollars." Lidia's puppet said pleasantly.

Lidia somehow knew how much money he had left, Felix thought, she was stressing the words to imply something there, there was no way that was a coincidence.

"Very well, I would like to purchase this information," Felix said plainly, making sure to keep his voice level.

The puppet clapped its hands again and took the card he held out towards it, she ran it through the machine the same type as the one in the Collectors building, and he entered his code at the prompt, Lidia's puppet handed him back his card and gave him another smile filled with needles.

"Thank you for your business, the identity of the one that placed the bounty is the leader of *this* Undergrounds Collectors; Jasper Cantrell," Lidia said pleasantly. "In the interest of turning you into a repeat customer, please allow me to give you some additional details; free of charge," Lidia said happily and continued. "The leader of this branch of the Collectors is currently in the city and he has scheduled an important meeting within the Collectors building at 07:00 AM, two days from now."

Felix stared at the thing, as it walked back onto the enormous finger, retreated across it adroitly to reach the palm, and then spoke one last time.

"I will also tell you this; You are not the only one who was seeking his location," Lidia said brightly.

The hand receded into the darkness, over the course of a very long minute.

They left the building without delay after that, and Felix refused to stop until they were at least several blocks away, but even then he knew, they were still within Lidia's reach, and the reason why nobody walked down that particular street suddenly made a lot more sense.

Mia hadn't said a thing since we had left the building, having been scared into silence, Felix completely understood her reaction because he was feeling much the same, and Remi wasn't any better off, eyes darting around at every movement in its periphery as if expecting a large hand to come grasping out of a dark alley.

Felix flinched as he remembered that Remi had been mangled by the large green hand of that bounty hunter *yesterday*, it was likely that Lidia's horrifying size had brought that back right back to the surface. Felix immediately joined the monster in looking down every single alleyway they passed just in case they did return.

Jasper Cantrell, Felix spun the name around in his mind.

He knew the identity of the person who had placed the bounty now, he also knew *where* the man would be and exactly *when* he would be there. It was an opportunity that Felix would likely not have again, as Lidia had said that Jasper was 'currently in the city' which left the implication that the man regularly *left* it. If Felix didn't get this settled now before Jasper left the city, how long would he have to avoid the hunters before Jasper might come back again? Felix didn't know, and he wasn't willing to take the chance.

Either way, Felix had gotten what he had come for, and the moment he could act wasn't for another two days. He would need to be able to get to the building by then, that meant leaving his home at some time earlier given the time it took to get back the Underground. Then he would need to either get inside the Collector's building, and wait for Jasper to arrive, or try and blitzkrieg it after the man had already appeared.

The building likely had guards or some kind of security force, so Felix probably wouldn't be able to just rush in without having to fight through every person in the building. It was a strange situation, in which every single person in the Underground had an unknown ability and an unknown stat distribution, but likely every single person would be physically stronger than him by a large margin, enough that they would be able to kill him with a single attack, a normal human could hit hard enough to kill someone, what could a person do with enough strength to dig grooves into concrete, like that man with the shield? It was almost as if everyone in the city held a gun and he had to make sure not to get hit.

Felix frowned, he needed to sit down somewhere quiet and figure out a plan of attack.

Going back to his apartment seemed like a waste of time, there had to be places he could find to stay for a couple of nights in the Underground right? He thought for a moment before turning to Remi keeping his eyes on the ground.

"Is there anywhere to stay in the Underground for several nights?" Felix asks quietly.

Mia had finally bounced back and joined the conversation before Remi could answer.

"We're staying here? That's awesome, where though?" Mia said excitedly, without even a hint of shame she had invited everybody along for the ride.

Felix couldn't believe how confident she was, he couldn't even dream of doing something like that, he cringed back from the thought of it, but

Remi just smiled and waited until Mia had finished before answering the unasked question.

"There are taverns on almost every and road if we were to choose one close to the Collector's building Mia could monitor it with her power," Remi said pleasantly.

The reasoning was solid and made it even harder for him to think of telling them both that he wanted to go alone, the tactical advantage that Mia could provide was immense.

"Finally I get to do something!" Mia said happily.

Felix couldn't find it in himself to mention that it would probably be incredibly boring just watching people stand around for hours, but Remi would be there and they would be there to keep each other company.

Felix's next pressing issue was money, he was now more or less completely broke, and he needed some way of making at least enough money to stay in a tavern for a couple of nights.

"What is the fastest way I can make money? Lidia asked for everything I had left." Felix explained quietly.

Remi looked back at him with a strange expression, and Felix quickly looked away feeling stupid for asking a former-slave about jobs to make money, he was an idiot.

"I have money, how much is a room for the night anyway?" Mia said easily.

Felix didn't reply feeling suddenly useless he couldn't even afford a room to stay in, he would need to find something very soon because having someone else offer to pay for his room because he couldn't afford it felt *terrible*.

As soon as he got back to the surface he would be looking into where all the banks in Saltwall City were located and finding out if crime actually did pay. The money was insured so as long as he was quick enough he could use to buy a property or something in the Underground and then trade that property back for less money than *wasn't* stolen. He *hated* the loss of control that this represented, he didn't want to rely on others and the feeling of humiliation clawed in his chest.

Felix was too busy lambasting himself to register what Remi had said in reply.

"That's easy! Let's go find a tavern then." Mia said happily and strode off down the street with Remi following along beside her.

Felix sighed and followed them both feeling abruptly miserable.

Mia and Remi found one quickly, that wasn't too far from the target's prophesied location and Felix stood awkwardly away from the other two as they spoke to the owner of the tavern, when they had finished haggling, they were given a single key and told to head on upstairs to room number twenty-nine. Felix told them to go on ahead and broke off to use the bathroom., and quickly found the bathroom by the sign hanging above the door and did his business.

Felix wondered about how strange his life had become in just a few short days, he had rarely spent time anywhere but at the Golden Salt Hotel working, or at his apartment on his own, and now he couldn't seem to find a moment of peace, he was caught in a whirlwind that was far above his ability to handle. Things had seemingly worked so far, but he knew it wouldn't last for long, he would mess up soon, he always did, only this time two others might end up getting hurt instead of just him.

He washed his hands in the sink and studied the man in the mirror, his pale face stared back at him, with all its flaws and imperfections, his hair was too long by the Hotels standards and looked like it hadn't been brushed in days because it hadn't.

"Are you going to be like this forever?" Felix accused the mirror.

The mirror didn't reply, and so sighed and turned away from himself in disgust.

Mia and Remi had continued onto the room that they had rented, and they had been asking about Remi's life as a servant when he had excused himself, so he took his time heading back to give them enough time to talk about anything they didn't want him there for.

The room they had selected supposedly had four beds; all singles spread across the length of the room, or some strange reason that Felix couldn't understand they didn't do single rooms *or* three bedrooms; only two beds, or four, so if you were a party with an odd number you had to either undersupply beds or oversupply them.

They had been offered a two-bedroom first, and Felix had been extremely uncomfortable with the idea, so they had ended up with a four-bedroom instead. Felix wondered if this was a way for the tavern to pry more money from the customer's hands, it certainly seemed to work. He meandered back to the room, before stopping to lean against the wall opposite the room labeled twenty-nine remained there in the hallway just thinking about everything that had happened unwilling to knock on the door.

A couple of minutes later the door abruptly opened to reveal Mia grinning at him, and Felix found himself once again embarrassed, this time for having been caught lingering outside the door like a coward. Mia stepped back and held her arm out behind her and he awkwardly stepped past her and into the room.

There were indeed four beds, and he made sure to choose the empty bed that was closest to the door to keep an empty bed between him and the other two. Mia had already spread out her things all over the place somehow, and her choice of bed was obvious. Remi was watching him in clear amusement from the other bed which must have been her choice. Felix laid back on his bed and stared at the ceiling before feeling strangely vulnerable being the only person laying down and immediately sat back up.

"Why were you just standing out in the hall?" Mia said amused after he had sat back up.

He didn't answer, instead, he crossed his arms and tilting his head back to study the pattern on the ceiling drawing a 'pfft' noise out of Mia before she turned back to Remi.

"What was I saying before?" Mia wondered aloud.

Remi glanced over at him once and he looked away.

"You mentioned that your mother had grown quite ill," Remi replied carefully.

Felix felt a distant pang in his chest, thinking of his own mother, long since passed.

"That's right, she was sick, for a really long time and spent most of her days in the hospital because of it," Mia said distractedly while staring down at the golden leaf on her hand. "I was always visiting her after school, and then when I finished school, I made sure to see her every day after work,"

Felix covertly began studying her face and tried to decipher the strange mixture of happiness and sadness that was present.

"She died at the start of last year, and I never met my dad, so she was all I had in the world," Mia said quietly,

Mia's smile had slowly disappeared by this point, and he noted that her eyes were growing wet.

"I wish I had found this place back then," Mia said quietly.

Felix could guess what she was thinking about, bringing her mother to someone with a mark and a healing power, like the old man in the market might have been enough to save her. Felix felt his stomach twist in empathy, what a wretched feeling that must have been, finding a place that had the power to heal your loved ones, but having arrived far too late for it to have made a difference.

Mia wiped at her eyes and laughed suddenly.

"She was amazing you know? Always so optimistic, always going after what she wanted with everything she had and encouraging me to do the same." Mia said brightly, eyes still wet. "I always wanted to be just like her, she was totally my hero."

Mia's smile lit up her face as she thought of the woman who had clearly meant so much to her, and she pushed herself to her feet before stepping closer to Remi.

"She always told me to just *take* the world by the *horns*,' Mia laughed, before grabbing Remi by the horns. "Come here world! I've got you now!"

The look of shock on Remi's face was one of the funniest things Felix had ever seen, and then Remi abruptly descended into giggles as the two started to wrestle with each other. Remi managed to flip over onto her stomach in her attempt to escape and had her face half pressed into the mattress as she stretched out a hand to Felix.

"Felix, help!" Remi laughed.

Remi quickly started thrashing as Mia abruptly switched to a merciless tickling and Felix couldn't fight down the smile that was spreading onto his face, so he turned around instead so they couldn't see it.

"Felix!" Remi squeaked at his betrayal.

Felix listened to the two of them wrestle for a while before Remi eventually managed to gain the upper hand and it was soon Mia who was begging for help, but eventually, they both had to stop having grown tired and out of breath, and simply returned to quietly talking on the bed.

Felix woke up suddenly, having accidentally fallen asleep on his bed at some point, and found that he was alone in the room, he closed his eyes and just enjoyed the quiet for a while. Felix had been tired for most of the day after his complete lack of sleep the night before, he had only just fallen asleep perhaps an hour before Mia had arrived at his apartment.

How long had he slept for exactly? It could only have been a couple of hours at most he thought, he checked his phone for confirmation and blinked when it said 4:00 PM, he had slept most of the day away, what a waste but he was feeling refreshed at least.

Two days until Jasper would appear, and he still hadn't come up with a plan on how to get inside the building, the best idea he had so far was to climb up to the roof of the building and then enter from there.

The Collector's building *was* the tallest building around for at least a block so he would have to go find the closest building in height and then use extend to lift himself, or find a rooftop that was of equal height and extent portion of *its* roof and then walk across it.

Everybody below him would probably be to see him do it unless he managed to get rid of the lights somehow, there was probably a time where they would click off, but if there wasn't it would be much more difficult. However, even if he got up there without being seen he would need to wait on the roof of the Collector's building until it was time for the meeting and that would only work if the security in the building didn't check the roof while he was on it.

If he *was* found on the roof then he was screwed, he might not be able to leave quickly, and he would be at their mercy. It was entirely possible that someone had a power like Mia's as well and would see him climbing the buildings or hiding on the roof and if they reported him, he would likewise be doomed, and it didn't even really have to be someone *in* the building that could see him if could be someone on the street or even a peacekeeper.

Felix was struggling to come up with anything worthwhile alternatives that would work any better than that, he was too weak for a frontal assault, although depending on exactly how strong Jasper and anyone else in the room with him was, even if he *could* surprise them the best plan might still fail if they were simply too strong to defeat through trickery.

Felix thought that the best time to cross to the building would be before the meeting started but he doubted it would be so easy, maybe he could get to him before he even entered the building, attack him on the streets somewhere if he could figure out which direction the man would be coming from, but that brought with it even more issues, even if the man did arrive when there was minimal traffic on the ground, there would no doubt still be *some* people around. They might assist the man, or the peacekeepers could just appear and do exactly what they were paid to do.

He needed to attack when Jasper had the fewest people possible around him, the ideal location would be in a room that was out of sight of anyone else, a room Felix could lockdown and not have to try and chase after the man, a room that was out of sight of the peacekeepers would also be nice.

Felix sighed again, having reached the same conclusion he had a hundred times before, he would have to attack during the meeting, he decided to think it over one more time, but before he could the door suddenly opened. Mia and Remi had reappeared and stepped into the room, with several trays of food in hand, Felix spent a brief moment thinking about pretending to be asleep, but Remi had already noticed his eyes were open.

Mia smiled at him and handed him one of the trays and Felix sat up and mumbled a thank you, feeling abruptly miserable again for not even buying his own food. Remi sat on the only bed that hadn't been claimed to face him and Mia sat down right next to Felix.

The tray had an assortment of foods, half of a chicken, several bread rolls, gravy, and a bowl of stew, that was a lot of food compared to what he normally ate, he wondered how much it had cost, he would have to ask later and pay Mia back for it.

Felix ate in silence while listening to the occasional exchange between the others and when the three of them were done eating, Remi broached the subject of Jasper.

"Have you given any thought to how we will gain access to Jasper Cantrell?" Remi asked pleasantly.

Felix almost sighed at the question, it's all he had been doing for hours and he still hadn't come up with a decent plan other than to hide on the roof and wait for the meeting, which suddenly sounded like an even more terrible idea than it had before when faced with the need to tell it to somebody else.

"I've tried, given the constraints and what I have at my disposal," Felix said quietly, barely above a mumble. "I was going to come in from above and wait on the building roof until the meeting started if I pick the right time I *might* be able to get up there their unseen.'

Felix stopped and waited for them to tear his plan apart, just as he had already done in his head at least ten times.

"Sounds good to me," Mia said cheerfully.

Felix glanced at her in exasperation but looked away when she noticed, Remi however gave some actual feedback.

"If they perform checks of the building or the roof, we could be seen, and if an unaffiliated third party sees us, they may also report our suspicious behavior to the peacekeepers," Remi said pleasantly, recanting the same weak points he had already found.

Felix noticed that there were a lot more uses of 'we' then he felt comfortable with, the situation was becoming dangerous now; it was now leagues above strolling through a *potentially* dangerous city before they knew about the bounty. This was walking *directly* into a building full of people who had killed, dismembered, and probably worse, things they would have no problems with repeating if we were caught.

"I don't see another way unless I attack before Jasper gets to the building," Felix said quietly.

Mia made a noise of understanding but didn't say anything; she *was* looking at him more closely, however.

"I see, which could end up much the same if peacekeepers became involved," Remi said thoughtfully.

"We also don't know what he looks like!" Mia said abruptly. "So, I wouldn't be able to find him for *us* to attack anyway!"

Mia had noted the distinction he had been making because she was putting a *lot* of stress on the word 'us.' Mia was right, however, somehow he had completely overlooked that he didn't know what the man looked like at all, Felix had just assumed he would *know* the man on sight for some reason, why *hadn't* he thought that? It was such an obvious point of failure that the fact that he had missed it. Felix drew his knees up to his chest and pressed his face against them, why was he so *stupid*.

"The roof does seem to be the best point of attack, entering from the bottom floor would put potentially hundreds of people between us and Jasper, perhaps to mitigate the chance of being found we can instead cause a distraction of some kind, and move to the roof just before the meeting?" Remi reasoned aloud.

Remi had clearly been following the 'I', 'we', 'us' hidden war that was currently going on. Felix had the same thought about a distraction earlier but discarded it because of the much greater chance of alerting the peacekeepers right as he would be attacking Jasper, besides it wasn't even certain he could even take the man down in the first place let alone if he accidentally drew more people to the area.

Felix was perhaps being overconfident, but he was *optimistic* that he might be able to pin the man to the floor and cage him like he had the other bounty hunters, but if he was too fast to target, or could avoid *being* targeted in the first place, like a power that made him intangible or a power that allowed him to teleport away from danger, he would just leave the area. Jasper was one of the leaders of an organization that potentially spanned *multiple* cities, he had to have had his pick of powers.

If I *did* attract additional attention during the assault and brought more people down on my head, I would have absolutely no chance, and Remi had realized it barely moments after speaking.

"Ah I see, if someone sees us setup or cause a distraction it increases the risk of bringing reinforcements down on us," Remi said curiously, studying his face intently.

"So we should just hide on the roof then?" Mia wondered aloud.

They were both looking at him to make the call, and being put on the spot made him distinctly uncomfortable, they were also apparently fine with inserting themselves into danger that they could easily avoid.

Felix nodded suddenly and forced himself to speak at a normal volume for the first time.

"It's the only plan I could think of, it will have to do I suppose," Felix said evenly.

Mia smiled at him, taking it as him including them in the plan but Remi was looking at him with an indecipherable look, no doubt realizing he hadn't agreed to anything of the sort. Felix had absolutely no intention of bringing them anywhere near the building and he decided quietly that he would lock them in the room or something to make sure they weren't able to follow him when the time came, the Collectors wouldn't go after them anyway, not if they already *had* Felix.

The bounty had only specified him after all.

Nine

They had watched the building for the entire next day and the rest of the night after that and even into the morning despite it remaining daylight the entire time outside the tavern, if they did turn off the lights it must have been at a much longer interval then a single day.

Mia had been continually searching the whole building from bottom to top with her shining golden eyes and reported a large number of people present in the building, going about their duties as if it were a normal office from the city above, and her eyes were looks dry from all the intensive use.

Felix had finally told the two of them to get some sleep, forcing himself to speak up about it, and surprisingly enough they listened to him, he had already taken another nap for most of the day, his sleep schedule was entirely disturbed and now he was wide awake at what should be the normal time to sleep. Felix stayed up the late hours of the night and through to the morning, browsing the internet on his phone which somehow still had signal even all the way down here.

There was a faint noise in the distance, Felix tilted his head and closed his eyes to hear it better, it almost sounded like glass breaking, and he found it interest that his hearing had improved so drastically. The fact that the noise had come from the same general direction as the Collectors building unnerved him for a moment.

They still had another day left before he was supposed to go to the meeting, but he glanced at his phone, anyway in case he had somehow missed a day, he hadn't, it was still 5:57 AM. It was almost time to wake the others. Felix frowned as there was another noise from the same direction, only this time it was almost like a whip cracking, and he started to have a bad feeling.

Felix slowly got off the bed and walked quietly past the two occupied beds to stare out the window, a red-light flickered briefly into the air before disappearing, what it was he was unsure, but it was almost directly above where the collectors building was.

Lidia had said that someone else had bought the same information, had they gone after the man a day early? Why would they? If he wasn't supposed to be there until tomorrow morning why go there *now*? What was going to happen now, was Jasper going to leave the city earlier? Would the meeting be pushed back?

Felix would have to check, he walked quietly past the bed that contained Mia and stopped to study her sleeping form for a moment, feeling abruptly guilty, they had stuck with him this entire time, despite only knowing him for two days, they had wanted to help him despite the grave danger they would be in, and got stuck in this mess because he was too much of a coward to tell someone no.

Felix thought he might never see either of them again if he left now, could he just leave them behind like this, without a word of thanks for tolerating him despite all of his flaws, could he leave without even saying goodbye?

Felix reached out his hand to almost touch Mia's shoulder, perhaps to shake her awake and then stopped, what was he *doing*? Felix *knew* that if they came with him they might die, and he *didn't* want that. It was simply because he couldn't ensure their safety, he couldn't bring them, so he steeled his resolve and pulled back his hand.

Felix moved quietly past the other beds towards the door, feeling his eyes sting.

Felix glanced back one last time and studied their sleeping forms for a moment before nodding, they didn't need to come with him, it had *nothing* to do with them. They would be fine here, and if he ended up failing, the bounty hunters wouldn't have any reason to go after them anymore.

Felix touched the door handle and twisted it silently, and paused at the sound of a bed squeaking but he didn't turn around.

"I thought you were going to crawl into bed with me for a minute there," Mia said softly, with a strange tone in her voice. "That's disappointing, way to make a girl feel wanted, Felix."

The other bed closer to him made a noise as well.

"Were you going to leave us behind?" Remi's said quietly.

Felix swallowed the lump in his throat and forced himself to speak.

"Someone's attacking the collectors building," Felix said quietly.

Felix stared hard at the wood grain of the door and blinked back the stinging in his eyes, Mia must have turned on her power because she gasped from her place on her bed.

"You should both stay here, I'm the only one with the bounty," Felix said quietly, before stepping out into the hall.

Felix shut the door behind him, and pushed his power into the doorknob, locking it into the doorframe, before he turned and ran down the hallway with an awful twisting in his stomach and feeling his eyes sting, he took the stairs three at a time and pushed open the door to the tavern, cut across the room and out onto the road,

Felix angled for the alleyway across the street and wiped at his eyes until he could see properly again, he reached the entrance of the alleyway and turned down it, heading in the direction of the noise, there was a fence at the end of it so he reached out with his power and twisted a part of the ground up in front of him.

Felix grabbed it tightly in his hand and it shot out of the ground, lifting him into the air and over the fence, he swung forward and stepped on a second branch of the pavement that shot out under his foot before riding it to the ground on the other side. Felix landed on the pavement with only a small stumble, having barely lost any of his momentum from the maneuver.

Felix exited the alleyway at his top speed, shot across the street and into the next alleyway directly across from the first, there was no fence to block him this time and he sprinted straight to the exit on the other side before whipping around the corner and coming to a stop with his hands on his knees, gasping for breath.

Felix took in his surroundings in an instant.

The glass frontage of the Collector's building was a shattered mess that was scatted half in the building and half on the street, there were bodies all over the ground in the lobby, and several on the pavement outside, all of them seemed to be bleeding a great deal and, in some cases, were already dead with massive holes in their bodies and limbs missing. Torn off, but not eaten he noticed, it likely wasn't the thing from the room. Whoever had done this wasn't hungry it would seem, they were simply after the experience, people and monsters were standing in front of buildings in small groups, pointing and looking worried.

A body was abruptly thrown clean out of the eighth-floor window with the sound of shattering glass and Felix watched as the man tucked into a tight roll, flipped backward once, and then tried to land on his feet on the pavement, the man's feet connected with the ground and his legs burst with an explosion of shattering concrete and blood. The man started screaming in pain a moment later, grievously injured but somehow still alive.

If someone was attacking *now*, it was for a good reason, Jasper might still be inside, Felix took off running towards the building, hiding on the roof was useless and would never work now so he jumped over the threshold of the building and into the lobby while trying not to slip on the glass. There was what he guessed was a receptionist cowering underneath the front counter holding a corded phone over her head and Felix rushed straight past the woman and past the elevator, having taken his oath seriously and straight into the stairs.

Felix stuck his torso over the railing and looked up there was a big enough gap between the sides of the stairwell for what he intended, with a twist of his power, a piece of the metal pipe that served as a railing extended upwards into the air, and he made a handle on the side of it, he reached out and grabbed the handle tightly and it shot upwards through in the middle of the stairwell.

Felix held it tightly and refused to look down, and listened carefully as he ascended, and as he approached the eighth floor he could hear crashing, so he extended the handle horizontally bringing him abruptly onto the stairs by a door.

Felix panted for a moment to regain his breath; he wasn't ready for all this running *at all*.

Felix stumbled through the door and only to find even more chaos then downstairs, the eighth floor was a single unbroken room, except for a divider on the far-left side, people were dead or dying all over the room and most of the room was damaged, a group of older men and women cowered beneath a large black table that dominated the divided section of the room.

No one that he thought was the attacker was in sight, and he still didn't know what Jasper looked like, it could be any one of these people. Felix opened his mouth to ask the people where they were when a man came slamming through the roof of the building, thick concrete slabs crashing down to the floor around him and he connected with the floor with a bang, cratering it.

Felix glanced over his shoulder at the sound of the door opening to make sure he wasn't about to get murdered only to find Mia and Remi stepping through the door panting for breath, he met Mia's eyes and flinched before turning his entire body away.

Felix stared at the man again who was still laying on the floor, the man's arms and legs were mangled badly and sat at abnormal angles, he was coughing wetly as well, with a great deal of blood covering both him and the floor beneath him but he seemed strangely aware and unbothered. Felix watched as he tried to stand up but failed, his legs completely unable to support him. Felix took a step towards the man and then immediately stopped as someone else dropped gracefully down through the hole in the ceiling, and he stared at where Naomi now stood over the man on the floor.

Why on earth was *she* here?

The familiar sense of dread had instantly returned when she had appeared but this time it was much, much stronger, almost at the level of the thing in the room, but strangely different. It hung in the air like an invisible force pressing down on everyone in the room. Naomi had cuts, burns, and hundreds of other tiny injuries all over her body, with matching tears in her dark, sleek segmented amour, but all of the injuries were all superficial at best.

Felix brushed past them all to focus on the only injury that *wasn't* there.

Naomi now had both of her arms somehow, the man on the ground said something, but Felix was too far away to hear it, but it must have been funny because Naomi started to laugh. It had become pretty obvious to him that Naomi was the *other* person who had bought the information about Jasper.

What was her reason?

Naomi clearly wasn't doing it to help Felix out, he had to of done something to her, was the man on the ground the one responsible for taking her arm and with it her power? Was this man *Jasper*?

Naomi turned suddenly and her gaze cut into him almost like a physical force before she looked up and to the left at nothing in the middle of the room, she suddenly disappeared and reappeared where she was looking and a person immediately dove out of her way from a spot where no one had been a moment before.

Invisibility, Felix thought or something like it.

Naomi glanced over the now visible man's shoulder and was suddenly directly behind him again but crouched on the floor, the man looked around wildly trying to reacquire her and vanished from sight again, but Naomi drove her hand straight into the air where the man had been, and a splash of red exploded into the air as the man reappeared with Naomi's hand sticking through his back and out of his chest. The man looked down at the hand sticking out of his chest and then went limp, sliding off Naomi's arm and hitting the floor with a wet slap.

Felix stared at the man in horror, this was *his* fault.

At the other staircase opposite him, two peacekeepers stepped through a door, different people from the ones he had witnessed the other day in the market and they immediately engaged Naomi in a furious melee, but she was seemingly much stronger than both of them casually brushing aside their attacks with the back of her hands and delivering crushing blows that broke limbs and a sudden twist that ended with one of the peacekeepers being tossed straight out of a window.

Naomi then vanished from her position and appeared again behind the second peacekeeper, but the man dove forward into a roll the second she was gone and spun on his feet swing his halberd at where she had been standing, but she was already behind him again.

Naomi reached over his shoulder and tore out his throat in an instant, and the man stumbled away from her choking and grasping at his neck before he fell to his knees on the floor. Naomi grabbed him by the back of his armor and tossed him as if he weighed nothing, straight out of the same window as his partner.

Felix watched and burned it all into his brain; everything that this woman had done since he had given her back her power was on him, he was responsible for *every single* injury and *every single* death if he had just stayed away from that café all of these people would still be alive.

Nobody else came into the room after that, and the oppressive atmosphere returned.

What surprised Felix the most about it all was the *ease* at which Naomi took them all apart, the sheer brutality of every action, and the absolute lack of any kind of remorse, they were simply obstacles in the path to whatever she wanted and they needed to be removed.

Felix suddenly understood.

The sense of dread whenever he was near her, her absurd strength, and willingness to kill, he had seen it before in one other place, with the thing in the room. It was so obvious in hindsight that he couldn't believe he had somehow overlooked it. Naomi was a Sin, one who had somehow *lost* her mark.

Felix had helped her regain it.

One of the people hiding under the table on the left side of the room scuttled out and stood up from before thrusting his hands in our direction, and the room exploded in response, crushing force smashed into the walls, the floors and everything else in the room, the roof partially collapsed, and Naomi reappeared behind the man completely unharmed by the attack. When the man's body hit the floor and his head rolled underneath the table, the rest of the elderly business people started screaming but made no further move to attack her.

Felix had barely managed to create an angled area of the floor to hide under when the roof had collapsed and a chunk of concrete half as big as a car rested precariously on the edge of it, he reached up and pushed it gently and it fell away from him further into the room with a startling loud crash.

Naomi turned to him at the noise.

A piece of rebar abruptly snaked past his feet and along the floor making sure to keep out of Naomi's sight and heading towards the people under the table, it circled around the table once before rising into the air, Felix glanced over at Remi who had moved further into the room and was standing next to the origin point of the rebar and noted that Mia was stuck with her leg trapped under a large piece of concrete with her necklace once again completely depleted.

Naomi noticed the wall of rebar as it reached the roof, with a frown on her face, before she turned back to look at them and a crushing wave of something rolled over him and Felix immediately spoke up before she decided to murder Remi.

"Naomi. I didn't expect to find you here." Felix said languidly, using the razor focus that her killing intent had granted him to think faster than he ever had before.

His mind raced through scenarios that all ended with all of them dead or in pieces, what had Naomi said about Sins?

They were driven by there most prominent desire or trait, it consumed them; Naomi had still felt dangerous even when she had lost her mark, she had still been driven by those same traits, just not as strongly.

What was Naomi's trait? Was it important?

"Felix, Felix, Felix," Naomi said brightly, with a terrifying smile on her face. "I see we have a bit of a *conflict* of interest going on!"

Naomi gestured at the man with the broken limbs, who had somehow despite his terrible injuries had managed to sit up, and Felix managed not to react at the confirmation that this was indeed Jasper Cantrell. The bulk of his mind was still calculating exactly how he could get the three of them out of this alive.

"It would seem so; Say, you wouldn't mind waiting for him to lift my bounty before you murdered him, would you?" Felix asked disinterestedly.

Jasper turned to stare at him from his place on the ground for the first time with a look of complete disbelief on his face, but Felix could see a flash of recognition shoot through his eyes but quickly disregarded it as unimportant.

Felix thought back to when he had met Naomi in the café, he had seen something in her face when he had insulted her the first time they had met, the expression had not been hatred, anger or disgust; it had been contempt.

Naomi thought others were beneath her, and she was right at least in regards to him if Felix was being honest, but despite all of her intelligence and cunning she was still driven entirely by something, and it might very well have been her pride for all he knew, a need to be superior? A need to win? Felix just needed to figure out how to weaponize it, to use it to capitalize on a single moment so they could all live.

Naomi laughed suddenly like what he said was the funniest thing she had ever heard and Felix switched mental gears.

Naomi's power was an Explorer's ability that was based on line of sight, she could move from one point in space to another almost instantaneously, but she *had* to pass through all the places in between, she couldn't move through obstacles, she was still physically present during transit, she could move from a standing position to a crouch, so there was some degree of reposition that was possible for her while in transit, but only a little otherwise she would be appearing in mid-attack.

"Sorry, I don't think I can hold myself back at this point," Naomi laughed.

Felix saw her glance at Remi and he immediately turned to warn the monster, but Naomi was already in a crouch directly behind Remi, Naomi rose from her crouch in a perfectly smooth motion and was already drawing her leg back in a kick, her leg flicked forward at obscene speeds that I couldn't even begin to track and just barely connected with the tip of the thick wall Remi had created directly between them.

Naomi's kick tore through it like it was wet paper, only slowing just enough that when it connected right in Remi's back it didn't tear the monster in half, but instead sent monster bouncing across the room, and leaving craters in the ground before she crashed bodily into the wall on the opposite side of the room. Remi coughed once but didn't otherwise move from its position half-buried in the wall.

The kick had landed right in the back, that had to be a broken spine at least, Felix thought in horror. Naomi tilted her head to the side and looked at him with a sick grin on her face and Felix immediately ducked down behind the massive piece of concrete next to him to keep it between Naomi and himself and she started laughing like it was the funniest thing in the world.

"Coward!" Naomi taunted, still laughing.

They both knew that she could appear above him in an instant, but *he* also knew that she wouldn't rush things, she would draw this out, Felix had held an advantage over Naomi for *days* and she wasn't the type to just end it all in an instant, she was going to savor it. Mia made a strangled noise from where she was stuck near the door and tried to yank her foot again but failed.

"Come out, come out, come out!" Naomi sing-songed, and stepped noisily towards him.

Felix took a deep breath and let it out slowly.

"Naomi!" Felix said sharply.

The second he heard her stop walking he reached down and pulled off his shoe.

"I *know* you're in there, somewhere," Felix said seriously, not believing a word of what he was saying. "I'm going to save you, so don't be afraid."

"*Idiot.*" Naomi hissed, scathingly. "Do you think this is a movie? That I'm some damsel in distress that needs saving? That you're my knight in shining armor?"

Felix pulled his sock off and put his foot in his lap before he activated his status silently, and it appeared in a soft golden glow.

"I *missed* being like this," Naomi laughed, "It's the greatest feeling in the world!"

Felix dumped all his twenty points into perception, hoping it would be enough he just needed to know a single piece of information *when* she was going to appear, he already had a good guess of *where*, he had already come up with and discarded a hundred plans, and he was sure they would have all ended with his death, and he *couldn't* just fill the room full of spikes, well technically he *could*, but there were still many people who might get hurt or killed.

They were laying on the ground everywhere and not all of them were completely dead when the points took effect, and the world suddenly changed before him, revealing much more of itself, he could hear the labored breath of some of them and see the small rise and fall of their chests.

Felix could see *so much* that he couldn't before, he could see Remi's chest moving up and down slightly, in the reflection of the unshattered window across the room, he could tell where Naomi was standing based on her breathing.

"I thought you had figured it out," Naomi said amused, taking a single step closer taking her time. "I thought I was going to have to hunt down that girl you're with to actually get a mark, but don't worry, I'll get to her in a moment."

Felix took a deep breath and stood up slowly, she was only a couple of meters away from him now staring at him with eyes like shards of ice, Naomi fought like a predator, she didn't attack from the front but only from a position where she had the advantage, she found a moment of weakness and then struck, bringing them down in a single efficient attack.

Remi's power had been barely enough to slow Naomi's kick down just enough to stop the attack from being lethal, and Remi had *much* higher stats then Felix did. There was *no* way that he would be walking away from even a single attack from her, he would only have a single try to get it right.

Felix had noticed something since he had stepped into this room, every single time Naomi had used her power, it was to appear directly behind of whoever she was attacking, she *always* reappeared in a crouch, it had to be something to do with making herself small enough to avoid obstacles, she would rise from her crouch and deal a punishing attack to inflict grievous damage upon them.

Remi had realized the same thing Felix had which was how Remi had managed to partially block her kick, the wall had already started to rise from the ground as soon as Remi had seen Naomi disappear from in front of her.

Felix and Remi's power were both quite similar on the surface, they both made things grow and warp or change, but there were some core differences; Remi's power kept the same durability as the origin of the material, but Felix's power made the material unbreakable, neither was better than the other, and they both had their strong points; Remi's power was far more versatile, the base range it could affect initially was *far* greater, and the things under its control could change direction without having to create a new segment. It had both an incredible defensive and offensive use, but there was one area where Extend was completely uncontested; it was much, much faster.

So when Naomi disappeared from in front of Felix, he had already begun extending spikes from the ground directly behind himself straight up into the air, which pierced through the roof and into the sky in an instant, something warm and wet splashed on his still bare foot and when Felix turned around, Naomi was dead.

Felix was still for a long moment before he managed to bring himself to slowly retract the thin spikes and slowly lowered Naomi's body to the floor, a feeling suddenly rushed from his foot and through his entire body; his knees went weak and he collapsed into a convulsing mess.

It was the same feeling he had felt when he had leveled up, only multiplied tenfold, he heard Jasper gasp quietly from his place nearby, a corresponding noise from Mia, and even a soft intake of breath from Remi across the room.

Felix could suddenly hear too much, the muffled voices of the people behind Remi's wall sounding loud but like they were underwater. Felix could see the reflections from the windows showing a hundred perfect replications of the room and his eyes abruptly focus through the glass and he could see a person walking towards their desk in a distant building, hundreds of meters away with perfect clarity.

His stat growth, Felix realized belatedly.

His Perception had increased dramatically from however many levels he had just gained, he held his head in his hands, he almost felt as if he had been blind before, there was so much he had been missing, he could hear a group of people ferrying the injured and dead from the bottom floors, but nobody would go higher than the third.

Felix dragged himself to his feet and stumbled over to Mia, who was still trying to lift the slab off her leg, and with a moment's effort, he used Extend to tip the concrete up and away from her with the help of a floor-post and helped her slide out.

"Are you alright?" Felix mumbled quietly, as he helped her stand up.

"I'm okay," Mia said weakly, as she stared down at the growing puddle of blood.

Felix turned away from her and walked past Naomi's body and across the room, Jasper watched him pass without comment, and he could feel Mia following him through the vibrations in the floor, there was an odd pattern in the floor generated by her walking, after a moment he realized she was limping. Felix approached Remi's broken body and the monster's eyes followed him as he came over, he managed to carefully pick Remi up and slowly moved back to the center of the room near Mia, to place her gently onto the ground next to her.

Felix stood again and turned to Jasper.

"This would be the part where you remove the bounty you placed on me," Felix said quietly, staring the man straight in the eyes.

Jasper stared back completely without fear, despite his mangled limbs.

"I have nothing to fear from you," Jasper said with a choking laugh. "You may have been able to beat her durability, but you *won't* be able to beat mine, my power works on a rule, and I know for a *fact* that you don't have the requirements to beat it."

Jasper coughed for a moment.

"You can't inflict any damage on me at all, the worst you could do would be to through me out of the window, and I'd *easily* survive that, I'll just wait for the peacekeepers to drum up the courage to come to get me."

Felix stared at Jasper for a long moment considering the words before slowly reaching down and touching the floor next to the man's arm with a finger. A needle-thin section of the ground extended upwards and passed through Jaspers' forearm with no resistance at all. Either Extend's strange invulnerability bypassed whatever rule Jasper's power supposedly worked on, or he was full of shit.

The spike exited right next to the golden leaf that adorned the man's arm.

Jasper gaped down at the spike in his arm in complete disbelief, before he tried to yank his arm away and gasped as it tore a larger section of his flesh.

"On second thought, how about we get rid of that bounty?" Jasper said with a pained grin. "There's a phone in my left pocket, hopefully, it hasn't been destroyed."

Felix glanced at Mia and her eyes shone with her power before she nodded, it likely wasn't a trap so he reached down and took the phone from Jaspers's pocket, it looked rather scuffed but was miraculously still functional.

"The passcode is 7882342, go to the contacts list, it's under 'Lidia'," Jasper said worriedly, watching the blood leak out of his arm slowly.

Felix followed the directions before ringing the number and the phone rang three times before the puppet answered.

"Hello Felix, I see you have managed to find Jasper." The puppet said pleasantly.

Felix couldn't find it in him to care how she could have possibly known who was ringing, Jasper coughed before speaking loud enough for Lidia to hear.

"Please remove the bounty down Lidia, it's no longer needed it would seem," Jasper said evenly.

Mia had knelt next to Remi and was stroking the paralyzed monster's hair gently.

"Very well, the bounty has been removed, there will be a two-month cooldown period before you can place another bounty on this target, I hope you understand," Lidia said pleasantly.

Jasper couldn't what Lidia said so Felix repeated it out loud.

"Yeah, I understand," Jasper sighed.

"Thank you, Lidia.' Felix said quietly.

"You're most welcome, you *are* a valued customer!' Lidia said pleasantly before she hung up.

Felix placed the phone back into Jaspers's pocket, before reaching down and pulling the man's wallet out, he thumbed it open and took two of the hundred-dollar bills, but left the many, many more behind, before replacing the wallet and standing up.

"Help, somebody. I'm maybe, kind of being robbed, somewhat." Jasper said deadpanned.

Felix just stared down at the man for a moment, about everything that had happened to bring him here.

"If you place another bounty on any of us, I'm going to kill you," Felix said quietly, before turning away.

Felix knelt to pick Remi back up and Mia helped him stand, even though she needed some help, Jasper didn't say anything this time and simply watched as they hobbled toward the elevator and Felix stepped inside without comment.

As the doors slowly shut, Felix made sure to burn the image of Naomi's body into his mind.

They rode the elevator down to the bottom floor and when the doors opened it revealed a line of peacekeepers standing at the ready in the lobby, but they made no moves in haste.

"The threat has been dealt with," Felix said quietly, "There are people upstairs in need of immediate medical assistance."

One of the peacekeepers from the side stepped forward and addressed the others.

"He's telling the truth, get upstairs and secure the area, once we have the all-clear we will bring medical up." The man said clearly.

The other peacekeepers immediately started rushing to the staircases on either side of the room at speeds he was sure he wouldn't have been able to follow ten minutes ago, and even then it was still difficult.

The leader of the Peacekeepers pointed behind him at the medical tent that had suddenly popped up across the street since he had been upstairs, it had a red cross on the front and a familiar old man was grinning and holding his pot out at people.

Felix headed straight for the man, hyper-aware of every movement of every person around him, but no one made a move towards them, and he joined the queue to the tent, five people and five bursts of pink light later and they were at the front. Felix lowered Remi down to the man and he reached out and touched Remi on the arm without even waiting for payment, and just like that Remi was completely healed. Felix sighed as he helped Remi stand up, and then stepped aside to allow Mia to receive her burst of pink light, she shook her leg out before putting pressure on it and smiling.

Felix reached and dropped one of Jaspers's notes into the pot and the old bastard grinned up at him. Felix turned and walked away without saying a word, or bothering to wait to be healed by the man, instead, he started in the general direction of the tavern.

It was almost funny Felix thought, that after everything that had happened in the last few days, all of the violence, death, and dismemberment he had seen, and it had all been fixed with a single conversation, a phone call, and Naomi's death.

Felix tried to think about what would have happened if Naomi hadn't attacked when she did, would they have been killed by all the people in the building? Without the overwhelming force she had brought to the

Collectors, would this have worked? Felix didn't think so, and he wasn't so arrogant to believe what little of a plan he had managed to think of would have still worked, not after what he had seen inside.

Felix had felt strange ever since he'd killed Naomi, he could feel laconic energy to everything around him, every motion a person made seemed almost sluggish, he swiped his hand out in front of him, but it just looked like normal to him, but he knew that wasn't the case, it was just that his Perception was a great deal higher than his Speed despite both having increased, he would have to even them out with his free points later.

Felix entered the tavern and walked straight past the bar, up the stairs and he found room twenty-nine and opened the door which was still locked with his power, he walked straight to his bed and fell face down on it noting that they had escaped by simply exiting through the window.

He really was an idiot.

Felix heard the others return a little while later, but they didn't disturb him and for that he was grateful, he was incredibly tired now, despite the overwhelming rush of adrenaline that was only now finally starting to bleed away, it was exhaustion brought on by to much mental strain, rather than anything physical.

Felix had killed a person; he felt the corner of his eyes sting, so he closed them tight, everything had felt strangely distant until now, and now he could feel everything rushing back into focus, Felix stayed face down on the bed and didn't move for a long time.

Felix awoke several hours later, but he didn't move straight away, he just listened.

Felix could faintly hear the employees in the tavern below talking amongst each other quietly, he could hear the breathing of two people in the beds that belonged to Mia and Remi, he could even hear the snoring of a person across the hall and down one room.

Felix sat up and finally opened his eyes, the world looked so much more real then it had yesterday. The artificial light that kept the Underground illuminated cut through the open window and lit up the room in a warm glow.

It almost felt like sunlight on his face, but just slightly off.

Felix could hear people walking past the tavern on the road, and he saw a flash of movement cut across the window, a bird, flapping its wings but the small instant that it was in view seemed to last a strangely long time. Felix pulled his foot into his lap, he realized belatedly that someone had removed his other shoe while he was asleep, either Mia or Remi, but he didn't feel bad, he just felt empty.

Felix activated his status and stared down at it.

Forty-three levels, that was what this system had deemed equivalent to Naomi's life, and the value of his own life had increased proportionally, it was almost as if he had stolen her life force to fortify his own.

Felix had been level four this morning, and now he was level forty-seven, he wondered exactly what the calculation had been to arrive that that number, Naomi would have needed to be at *least* that level.

No, Felix thought suddenly, that wasn't near enough, Naomi had killed half a hundred people at least in that building, and she had left that same amount again injured, Remi, Mia, and Jasper had all been alive there as well.

All *three* had leveled up, probably *multiple* times. Felix was willing to bet that every single person that had still been alive had gained at *least* one level when she died, and he assumed that he must have gotten a larger share than the rest because *he* had killed her, and the system *awarded* him a larger share of her life force. Naomi would have likely been at *least* over level one hundred, but probably much higher.

He was as strong now, Felix realized, well, maybe not *strong*, but *fast* and *perceptive* at least.

Felix had two hundred and fifteen points to spend, he could peel back even more layers of the world with increased perception, become exceptionally durable, gain the strength to crush concrete or become faster than a car, he could become a specialist or a jack of all trades and a master of none.

Felix stared down at his foot and tried to decide, in a few short minutes how he would shape himself for the future, he thought about the people he had witnessed that had to have been at a high level. Jasper had a power based on his durability stat, and his comments on the rule indicated it was something he had put a lot of his points into.

Jasper had to have had a higher than normal durability, and Naomi had torn him apart just like everybody else, it had just taken a little bit longer to get through that durability. Felix wondered what her level had actually been, he wondered what she had been like with her original skill at her disposal.

Naomi had exactly *one* day to get used to using that movement ability, and it had been long enough for her to decimate the entire building's worth of high-level people, if she had longer to get used to it, she probably wouldn't have fallen into the trap of attacking the same way every time.

From her perspective, with her overall power, it must have felt like crushing ants even the Peacekeepers, veteran warriors from what he understood, had been taken apart in a matter of moments, their strikes brushed aside by her overwhelming strength and the ability to set up for a kill shot with a simple twitch of her power.

Felix knew that there had to be monsters even worse than Naomi that walked the world, who could crush have crushed her front on without trickery, but even if he put every single point he had gained into durability, it would never be as high as someone with a stat growth that focused on it, or an ability that leveraged it like Jasper.

The same could be said for his strength, he gained *no* points in it naturally, and as a result, would lose most battles of strength even if he did put it all into it and there was no synergy with his ability there. It would be better to stack his advantages, Perception, and Speed.

Perception would allow him to gather information better and see attacks coming, but Speed would allow him to avoid them, his Perception would naturally increase at a high rate without ever having added to it and his power had gifted him with an ability that he could bypass Naomi's durability with, that could pierce even Jasper's vaunted durability with no resistance, there was only one choice he could make.

Felix was still staring off into space and thinking about everything when the others finally started to wake up. Remi stirred first, rising slowly up to a sitting position and looking around the room and Felix did his best to meet the monster's eyes and it was still just as difficult as before, but maybe not *quite* as bad.

"You're awake,' Remi said quietly, rubbing one of its eyes with a hand.

"Mm." Felix noised, watching Remi from his bed.

"I didn't mean to sleep so long," Remi added after a moment.

The quiet exchange was enough to wake Mia and she shot up to a sitting position as if she had just been shocked awake, Felix stared at her in disbelief wondering how anyone could possibly wake up so quickly.

"I think we were all worn down," Remi said softly.

Mia turned at the monster's voice and caught sight of both.

"You're both finally awake!" Mia said excitedly as if she had just found *them* waking up, and not the other way around.

Remi laughed at the comment and stuck out a very long tongue.

"Did you know you snore, Mia?" Remi said cheekily.

Mia's mouth dropped open in shock and she looked as if she had just been betrayed and Felix laughed at the expression and the two of them snapped their heads around to look at him and Felix trailed off unsurely at the sudden attention.

"You *laughed*!" Mia accused and pointed at him, Remi nodded in agreement before lifting a hand to point at him as well.

Felix flushed and flipped over onto his side to face away from both them and pulled the covers up over his head, embarrassed.

"Ah!" Mia noised in surprise at his sudden vanishing act.

"He escaped." Remi laughed.

Felix remained under his covers and refused to surface despite their taunting, and once they had given up on goading him out, he waited a bit longer before finally dragging himself out of the bed, and took a few quick steps towards the door his mind already racing.

Felix was going to need to find some sort of income now, especially if he wanted to change the world, Felix didn't he would still have a job as a bellhop now, Alistair would be pleased with least, he stopped at the door and rifled through his pockets for a moment until he found his wallet, he opened it and checked what he had left.

Only a solitary one-hundred-dollar Jasper-bill remained.

Mia and Remi watched him as he stood at the door in complete silence and Felix realized they were probably comparing his exit with the last time when he had locked them in the room and left them behind, Felix reached out and twisted the door handle.

"I'm going to get something to eat, are you two coming with me, or are you going to sleep all day?" Felix said quietly, before letting the sounds of squeaking beds, ruffled clothing, and cries for him to 'Wait!' wash over him.

Felix waited at the door with a smile.

Status
The Sage
Extend
Level 47
Durability: 5
Perception: 213
Strength: 5
Speed: 266
Points: 0

Other places to find my stuff!

Patreon - Elbowsnapper.

Online - Elbowsnapper.